About the Author

Elizabeth hails from West Cumbria in the UK. She was a voracious reader from a very young age but only started writing seriously in 2012 after a friend offered some encouragement.

She now lives in South Warwickshire with a very spoiled black and white cat.

Siren Spirit is her first novel.

Siren
Spirit

Elizabeth M. Hurst

ISBN-13: 978-1517191337
ISBN-10: 1517191335

www.lizhurst.co.uk

@LizHurstAuthor

Cover design by Design4Writers.com

Chapter One

October 1784

"Come on then, girl. No good standing in the shadows where we can't see you."

Despite her grey overcoat, Grace shivered by the door, the cold wind tearing at her skin through her dress and petticoats. It was warm inside the forge, at least. She shuffled towards the fire and the two men working there.

"Grace, I'd like you to meet Tom. He's going to be working with me from now on and living here with us. It means we'll have another mouth to feed, but it also means I can take on more work."

"Pleased to meet you, Miss," said Tom.

Grace looked from her father to the new face and held out her hand. "Hello, Tom."

His blue eyes were somewhat sunken in from the tanned skin. He had worked outdoors, that much was obvious, both from his muscular physique and his strength, which became apparent as they shook hands.

She longed to have skin which grew tanned in the sunshine, but she had been blessed with a translucent complexion, rather like her poor dear mother, a fact that made it difficult even now, several years after her death, for her father to look her in the face. Such a pretty face too, her dark hair framing delicate elven features. She remembered herself as a little girl, walking through the village with her mother and hearing exclamations of praise from the ladies.

She sighed inwardly. She knew her father was busy these days, not just with shoeing horses either, or with repairs to Mr. Thatcher's harrow and his other farm tools. They had started work on the canal nearby. Workers were forever turning up with broken pickaxes that had to be mended. Then there were the wagon wheels and iron tyres from the carts that carried out the dug earth. And of course these carts were drawn by yet more horses, all of which needed new shoes from time to time.

What really worried Grace, however, was her father's intention to have her married off to a nice young man as soon as possible.

This time the sigh escaped her lips, and she watched for a while as her father worked. She had always loved to watch him work, even as a small child. She had no fear of the dancing flames, the red-hot coke pieces or the yellow-hot molten metal as he removed it from the furnace with his tongs. Her favourite part came next. She closed her eyes to better appreciate the noise of the hammer striking the metal.

DING! DING! DING!

Tom rested for a moment against the wall of the forge, his arm leaning on the bellows to keep him upright. He also watched Joe Richardson working the glowing metal into shape. Sparks flew onto the blacksmith's leather apron as he knocked the clinker off the iron onto the floor. Tidying up the waste material would be part of his new job.

Grace turned her back on them and made her way back into the bad weather. "I'll put more broth on the stove for dinner, then," she shouted, just above the racket.

"You do that," her father shouted back, without looking up.

December 1784

Grace stood on the chair with a heavy heart. The lone candle was almost out but it still cast a subdued light across the cold, empty forge.

An image came to her mind from that first meeting with Tom; the way he had looked at her, and her father's nodding towards her. It all made sense now, but it didn't alleviate the heaviness in her heart.

It was some time after midnight. The fire had long since gone out, and they had both gone to bed an hour or so earlier, following their usual ritual of a couple of ales at the inn down the road. She had waited until she could hear them snoring before creeping downstairs.

Sorrow filled her soul. The rain battered the roof like an expectant drum roll and she shivered. She glanced at the letter she had carefully placed upon the workbench and a single tear rolled down her cheek. She checked the rope one more time and then, taking a deep breath, she stepped off the chair and into oblivion.

Chapter Two

May 2015

As the removals van drove away down the narrow country lane, Emma McVeigh allowed a deep, mournful sigh to escape her lips. As last she could be alone with her thoughts.

From her position, sat halfway up the stairs, she surveyed the scene. There were cardboard boxes piled everywhere. She knew she should really make a start on the unpacking but had little motivation or energy.

First thing's first though. A nice hot drink. Having dug out the kettle from the chaos earlier in the day to try and keep the removals guys happy, she made herself a steaming mug of soup and settled back on the stairs. She remembered her mum's advice: "Always keep a box of essentials handy and make sure it doesn't go in the van. Keep it with you so you don't lose sight of it."

Lily, her black and white cat, appeared at the bottom of the stairs and gave a tiny murmur. She joined her where she sat and nuzzled her ankles, seeking comfort and reassurance in the strange new territory. Emma stroked the velvet ears.

"Hey, Lily," she said. "It'll be nice here. You'll see."

The cat gazed up at her, as if she knew her mistress's words were more for her own comfort than anything else.

Retreating into her thoughts again, Emma wondered if she had done the right thing, moving to the country.

She had never lived in a village before. What if she hated it? What if she couldn't make any friends? Was she really ready to swap her taxi-and-takeaway lifestyle for a more sedate life?

In truth, though, she needed a fresh start. The divorce had been relatively straightforward but had nonetheless taken its toll. Fine lines were beginning to show around her jade-green eyes, which she knew were more the result of sadness than laughter.

"Take each day as it comes," her mother had said. "A broken heart just needs time."

How had she arrived here at this crossroads in her life? What had gone so wrong? She reflected on her marriage. They had been so happy, happier than she had ever thought possible. Was there anything she could have done to save it?

She drained the last of the soup from the mug and let out another sigh.

Meow.

"Are you hungry, Poppet?"

The cat gazed at her with expectant eyes.

"I know how it feels to be a single parent," Emma said, a wry smile appearing on her face. "Having to hold it all together for the sake of the kids." She lifted the cat into her arms and hugged her. "I need you to be my rock now, Lily. Can you do that?"

Meow.

The warm, purring mass of fur brought such comfort. Emma felt like a small child cradling her favourite teddy bear. She trudged through to the kitchen with Lily over one shoulder and then set her down on the floor while she prepared food and fresh water. She then crouched to stroke her companion as the cat munched her way through her favourite dinner.

A muffled chime rang out from one of the boxes in the hallway. Emma found her carriage clock and placed it on a small table. Already it was striking ten o'clock, although sunset didn't feel so long ago. She yawned. She had been on her feet all day and needed some rest. She could always unpack tomorrow.

Emma grabbed her overnight bag (another of her mother's tips) and headed upstairs to the master bedroom. Damn! She hadn't yet made the bed. Oh, well. It would have to do. She had barely enough energy to lift the duvet out of the large black bag. She dragged her weary body onto the bed and wrapped it round her, before curling into the foetal position and waiting for sleep.

Her husband had told her he didn't find her attractive any more. How could anyone say anything so cruel? Tears stung in her eyes at the recollection. Sadness enveloped her and she turned her face into the pillow, trying to hide from the world. Sleep was far away tonight and she lay awake, trying to control her breathing and slow her heart rate, which was still buzzing from the adrenalin-fuelled events of the day. Eventually, though, she drifted into a difficult sleep.

The cat was not sleepy either and perched on the windowsill overlooking the garden. A barn owl began its hunting trip from the trees opposite, its flight path perfectly illuminated by the light of the full moon.

Had Emma stayed awake, she would have witnessed Lily turn and hiss towards the room's interior, apparently empty but for her sleeping mistress.

In a large field at the other end of the village, Rob Thornton was locking up the Portakabin for the night. It had been a frustrating day, all told – paperwork to complete for the project, which was overdue, and the council was screaming at him to get the schedule back on track. The company had an obligation to get this first phase of houses up and finished as soon as possible so they could bring in some much needed revenue to complete the next phase of the development.

Rob recalled the labourers' reaction when he ran over towards the source of the shouting, the day the trouble started. The cries he heard weren't a sound you often heard from grown men. Sheer panic, that's what it was. One of the guys, Brian, had left the site that day, never to return. He was approaching retirement anyway. Rob had had to go round and visit him at home to deliver his last wage packet.

He looked up at the full, round moon. He had seen way too much of life to be affected by any old wives' tales. He strolled towards the pub where he stayed during the week. Home tomorrow, to his wife and kids. It had been a long and eventful week.

Chapter Three

Emma woke gently the following morning to the sound of birds chirping in the trees. Before even opening her eyes, she indulged herself with a full-body stretch, which brought her senses to life. She could feel the warmth of the late-spring sunshine streaming through her windows, bathing her in a comforting glow, like a ray of hope. Already this little cottage felt like home. The pale yellow of the bedroom walls reflected the summer sunlight and Emma felt as though a seed of optimism had been planted within her. From somewhere deep inside, she found the strength to smile. She remembered she had new oak furniture arriving in a few days, so that was something to look forward to. That was a good thing, the self-help books said.

"I believe I shall start with the bedroom," she said out loud.

Lily joined her on the bed to protest.

Meow.

"Oh, OK then. Breakfast first, I know. Come on then, Lily."

Navigating her way through the boxes, Emma made her way to the kitchen. Just as she had fed the cat, the doorbell rang. A glance at the clock made her gasp. Eleven o'clock. She had slept for hours!

She had barely opened the door when she was verbally assaulted.

"Do I presume correctly that the silver Ford Ka is yours? It's blocking my lane and I can't get out. Kindly move it as soon as possible. I'm already late for a meeting."

Emma stood still for a moment and stared at the man on her doorstep. She had expected a warmer welcome to the village, truth be told, but the look on the man's face did not give her cause to start any chitchat so she grabbed her keys, slipped on her shoes and ran out of the door.

"I'm terribly sorry," she mumbled, running down the steps. "I'll move it straightaway."

"Yes, please," came the stern response.

Emma didn't look up to meet the man's face. She was far too embarrassed at his having caught her in her pyjamas this close to noon, and at forgetting to move her car last night after the removals men had left.

She quickly moved the car and ran back into the house, mortified. What a dreadful start. So much for peaceful respite from the world in a sleepy little village. Apparently, her new neighbours were just as rude as her previous ones from the city. What a dickhead!

Emma spent the rest of the day moving some boxes into the attic for storage and unpacking others. Having moved house several times, she had become adept at carefully labelling everything to ensure minimum stress at this stage. This also meant she could start to feel settled and organised, which suited her sensibilities, and she very rarely lost anything.

In an attempt to feel like she was making a fresh start, she had sold a lot of the existing furniture and given a significant amount of things to charity. The food mixer, given as a wedding gift, some music CDs which reminded her of her ex-husband and a coffee table had all found themselves new homes. She couldn't bear the thought of being surrounded by things they had chosen as a couple, so she had kept as little as possible. Only two leather sofas and her beloved bookcases remained.

Unpacking books was never an odious chore. She found it satisfying on many levels. There was quite a selection of travel guides from various cities and countries she had visited. She liked to think her houseguests would be impressed by her being so well-travelled. City guides to Berlin, Rome and Paris snuggled up against phrasebooks and dictionaries. They proved that she was not the sort of girl who spent her holidays lying on a beach or in a pub before flying home again.

She was deep in among her Dickens and Hardy collections when there was a shrill screech from the bottom of the stairs. Her heart jumped in her chest; then she realised it was the old Bakelite telephone the previous tenant had left behind.

Must get that sorted out, Emma thought, noticing the cables that dangled down the steps, as she picked up the receiver.

"Hello?"

"Emma, it's your mother. How are you, dear?"

"I'm okay, thanks. I ..."

"Well, why didn't you call and let us know you were all right, then? Honestly! You know your father and I worry about you, don't you?"

"Yes, of course I do. It's just ..."

"I really wish you were more thoughtful sometimes." There was a difficult pause at the other end.

"So, how did the move go?"

Emma's heart sank. Her mother was well-meaning but she had a tendency to be rather overbearing. She also knew that her mother was still grieving over the breakdown of her marriage and felt that by contacting her daughter to offer advice on everything under the sun gave her some purpose.

Emma told her that the move had gone very well, thank you, and that both she and the cat were slowly settling in to their new surroundings without too much hassle.

"It's so quiet and peaceful here, Mum. You'll like it."

There was a pause.

"Hmmm. It's a shame Paul's not with you then. Maybe it would have done some good, you know?"

"Mum…" Emma rolled her eyes towards the top of the stairs, settling on the cat who returned her stare.

It's your mother, Lily seemed to say. *Give her a break.*

"I know, I know." Her mother was doing her best to be tactful, but it wasn't easy for her. "So, have you heard from him at all?"

"No, Mum, and I don't expect I ever will. And, you know, I'm okay with that. I need to move on."

"Right. Okay then." Another pause. "Well, I just wanted to check you were alright. Keep in touch, Dear, won't you?"

"I will, yes. Bye."

A wave of relief washed over Emma as she replaced the receiver. She loved her mother dearly but they didn't always see eye to eye and it had caused some tension over the years. Still, she was grateful for her wisdom at times. It just took some patience, that's all.

11

The mention of Paul had brought sadness back to the surface, and she hugged her knees to her chest as she sat on the stairs. She was neither upstairs, nor downstairs. "This is where my life is right now," she mused. "I am neither married nor single. I'm in a no-man's land; in an in between kind of existence, swimming in a sea of who-the-hell-am-I. I have absolutely no idea what my future holds. What do I have to look forward to?"

Meow. Mrrrrr. Lily cocked her head and gazed up at Emma.

"It's okay, Lily-cat." She stroked the furry head. At least Lily would never leave her feeling utterly neglected.

***

The doorbell wasn't such a shock this time.

"Hi. I wanted to apologise for my rudeness earlier. It was totally uncalled for. My name's Lewis, by the way. I'm your next-door neighbour, in case you hadn't realised."

Emma looked him up and down, this time without embarrassment. He had changed out of the suit he had worn earlier in the day and into faded jeans with a casual shirt. He was handsome, she noticed. The ice-blue eyes searched for a response from beneath a full head of dark brown hair. There was a little stubble, but nothing to hint at a predilection for the current facial hair trend which Emma hated so much.

He held out a hand and she shook it. His hand was warm; the handshake was firm but not too hard. A

12

bunch of nerves tightened through her stomach as he let go.

His smile caught her unawares. It lit his face and the coolness of his eyes appeared to turn warmer for a second. Inside her chest, Emma's heart did a little skip.

"Hi Lewis, I'm Emma," she said, smiling back.

"I realise you've just moved in so, by way of an apology, I wondered if you'd let me buy you a drink and some food at the pub? That is, if you don't have anything already organised?"

"Actually, I haven't had a chance to go shopping yet, so that would be lovely, thank you." Emma smiled again.

"Great, I'll pick you up at around seven o'clock ish?"

"Perfect. I'll see you then."

Emma was still smiling long after the door closed. It seemed her new neighbour wasn't such a dickhead after all. And he was good-looking too, which was an added bonus.

A dark feeling came over her, reminding her she wasn't ready for any kind of commitment to anyone. Her heart no longer belonged to Paul, but it required some TLC before she could give it to anyone else. Lewis would have to remain in the 'just good friends' category. For now, at least.

Lewis returned to his house with uncertainty hovering in his mind. Damn, his new neighbour was gorgeous. There was something in her eyes which told of a certain fragility which he found attractive. Thank goodness she had forgiven him his rudeness from the morning. It was a relief, but he didn't want to get involved with her, despite the attraction. Not after the last disaster.

Still, he could always use some new friends. Wasn't that why he had moved here? To get away from the facade of his previous lifestyle and find some genuine, more down to earth people?

Chapter Four

It was Friday evening, and the cosy village pub was packed. A few faces nodded in Lewis's direction as they wandered through to the dining area. A waitress showed them to the only free table and took their drinks order.

"I didn't realise this was a formal dinner date?" Emma smirked at Lewis, then looked down at her jeans in dismay. They were not the outfit she would have chosen for somewhere like this.

"Oh, they don't stand on ceremony here," he reassured her. "But the only way to get a table at the weekends is to book in advance, and I come here every week anyway. It's nice to have some company for a change."

She looked over the menu. "It all sounds lovely."

"I can recommend virtually everything. Especially this," he said, nodding to the bottle of wine the waitress was pouring into their glasses.

"A toast, I think. To your new home!"

They clinked glasses. Emma felt the liquid pour down her throat far too easily. "Oh, that's just what I need, after the day I've had," she said.

"I can well imagine."

Lewis raised a sarcastic eyebrow, which piqued her curiosity, so she cocked her head to encourage him to explain himself.

"I saw the removals guys yesterday, and something was conspicuous by its absence."

"Oh?"

"You have moved into an empty, unfurnished property with virtually no furniture."

An awkward silence fell for a few moments. Emma dropped her gaze towards the empty place setting on the table, willing the waitress to arrive and take their food order, saving her from further embarrassment.

As if sensing her unease, Lewis started telling his own tale.

It seemed he had moved to the village under similar circumstances. He hadn't wanted to work for his father in the family business so decided to move out of the City and into the countryside, seeking a more simple life. He was a keen painter and wanted to develop it further, hoping the relaxed pace of life would encourage his more creative side to manifest in his work.

By the time Lewis had finished his story, Emma was half a bottle of wine down and starting to feel a little tipsy.

Finally the food arrived. She hadn't realised how hungry she had been and tucked into her food with a rare enthusiasm. Once the fish and chips were devoured, she relaxed and sat back with a contented smile.

"That was delicious, thank you."

"I'm surprised you had the time to taste it," Lewis teased. "You must have been hungry. So, are you ready to tell your story?"

"My husband and I drifted apart really," she began. She couldn't tell him too much. Not yet. She recalled some of the grimy details and chose to tell the edited highlights. "It's been an emotional rollercoaster, to be honest. He just came home one day and told me he didn't find me attractive any more."

Tears pooled in her eyes but she managed to blink them back while taking another gulp of wine for courage. *Not here, not now. I hardly know him.*

"Shit. I'm sorry. You don't have to talk about it if you don't want to."

Lewis placed a tentative hand over hers. She desperately needed a friend to confide in, but she didn't want to make herself appear vulnerable either. She was stronger than that. Besides, she had moved here so she could start over. *Time to get a grip.*

"My friends have been great but they wanted me to move sooner. They say I haven't grieved properly yet." She rolled her eyes and gave a sarcastic grin. The emotion was threatening to overwhelm her again but she pushed it away.

"Well, I for one am very glad you've arrived," Lewis said.

He whispered something to the waitress as she removed their plates, and Emma took the opportunity to glance around the bar and restaurant a little more. The remaining customers were finishing their desserts. They would soon be alone save for the few stragglers in the bar at the front.

She need not have been concerned about talking to Lewis. He changed the conversation several times, and with skill, to avoid her dwelling on her past. He spoke of his painting and showed her photos of his work, which she admired. He also had a successful painting, decorating and odd-job business in and around the village and the surrounding area.

17

Lewis pointed out several characters in the bar - the headmistress of the primary school, Mrs. Sampson, and her husband, an accountant in the neighbouring town; Reverend Smythe; Lesley, who ran the convenience store was chatting to Clive, an elderly gentleman whose wife had passed away many years ago. The gossip was that he and Lesley had been having an affair for years but had never made it public.

These were the stalwarts of the village, the people who fought to keep its quaint English character in the face of the threat from a construction company.

The village had fought off Sirius Construction at first, after the first planning application included over a hundred new homes. After negotiations and help from local businesses, however, the villagers had conceded to more modest plans on the understanding that the developers would also provide amenities so that the village could cope with the rising population. According to Lewis, survey work was now complete, and they had started clearing the area and laying foundations for the first few houses.

Lewis offered Emma his hand as he walked her home to the cottage. "The parish council is campaigning for more street lamps," he explained. "But in the meantime, the path up to yours can be lethal in the dark."

She took it reluctantly at first, but after a few yards Emma realised she could barely see a thing and was glad of the support. Suddenly, she missed the hubbub and glow of the city. It was almost too quiet.

Lewis was the perfect gentleman as he wished her goodnight. It had crossed her mind that he may try and kiss her, and she had been worrying about how to handle the situation.

The cottage was quiet as she entered. Lily opened a single eye from her place on the sofa and decided it wasn't yet breakfast time, so went back to sleep. Emma didn't really want to spend the night alone but she realised that she had no choice. She was still not over Paul, and …

A whooshing noise interrupted her thoughts. She froze at the bottom of the stairs and looked up towards the source of the noise. On the landing, an old perfume bottle she had found was rocking to and fro, quicker and quicker, then came to rest exactly where it stood, on a small table overlooking the top of the stairs.

She stared, unblinking. All was still, save her heart, beating so fast it threatened to burst through her ribcage. The faint yet unmistakable scent of lily of the valley flowers wafted down the stairs towards her.

Standing still, Emma weighed up her options. Should she stay and wait for whoever might be upstairs to finish and come down? Or, should she go up and confront the intruder?

"Hello?" she managed to whisper.

The moments passed in a bizarre fashion; the clock ticked but Emma couldn't gather her mind sufficiently to have the faintest idea how long she stood there for. She stared at the perfume bottle. The fragrance had dissipated and the small glass receptacle was still, just as if nothing had happened.

No one answered.

A terrible thought hit her. Where was Lily? A tiny murmur came from behind her, and the reassurance of warm fur curling around her calves allowed her to let out the lungful of air she had been holding in.

She grabbed the nearest thing she could find to use as a makeshift weapon - an umbrella - and slowly climbed the stairs. Reaching the table, she picked up the perfume bottle and examined it. It had caught her eye on moving day; such a pretty little object – emerald-green cut glass with a stopper in the top. She shivered as she touched it and she felt light-headed. Regretting her slightly tipsy state immediately, she decided she had been imagining things and placed the bottle back down on the table.

With only slight wariness, Emma made her way to bed, with Lily following behind her. As her eyelids drooped, she resolved to try not to get spooked by stupid things. She lived in the country now. There were all sorts of strange noises and she would just have to get used to them.

Chapter Five

February 1784

Sunday, 29 February

Today would have been Mama's birthday. Oh, I do miss her so. I am in the parlour now, looking at her collection of books. She has signed her name, in her best handwriting, inside the cover of every one. Pa can't bear to let them go, but he does not approve of me reading them as much as I do.

My favourite stories are here. Robinson Crusoe and his Man Friday having such wild adventures. The tale of the boy Tom Jones is another. I have read these a dozen times each, I swear!

Mama was so clever. I remember sitting here with her, as she taught me my letters and numbers as a little girl. I remember Mama and Pa arguing because she wanted to teach me. Pa thinks only boys should know such things, but why must I not enjoy these books too?

Sunday, 21 March

It's late in the year for us to be still having a frost, I can tell you. It's meant to be the first day of spring, but I almost slipped on the icy cobbles on my way from the bakery with the breakfast bread. It turned out to be a beautiful day, though, in the end.

After my chores at home and with Pa at the forge after lunch, I went to call on Lucy. Her cousin Suzanne is staying with them. Poor lamb! Suzanne's parents were both killed just two months ago in a terrible carriage accident in London,

Lucy said, and her aunt has brought her here to rest and recover. It will be to get over the shock, I imagine.

It put me in mind of Mama again, and of why my dear Pa finds it so hard to look at me now I am older. I know he misses her, but I feel sometimes that I have almost lost my Pa too. I can't remember the last time I saw him laugh, or even smile.

Easter Sunday, 11 April

Well, what a lovely morning at church! So nice to see Lucy and Suzanne there too, looking so fine, both in their new frocks. I wish I could look the same in mine but I've never had a mind for all the fashionable ladies things. Mama always said I was to be admired for my brains because that is what's important in this world.

Suzanne's overbearing aunt has returned to London now and I notice she seemed much happier than the first time I met her. It surely makes her very much finer when she smiles too. She'll catch the eye of some suitor before long and be swept off her feet, no doubt.

Easter Monday, 12 April

I was so excited to be invited to visit Lucy and Suzanne for tea today. Lucy promised to find the best cups and saucers she could so that we could make believe we were ladies of standing, like that Lady Shotterham up at the manor.

Lucy brought some freshly baked cakes, and she sat and chattered on about Mr. James Postlethwaite, who has been paying her some attention, it would seem. She is most distracted by the whole thing. He seems a nice young lad, I suppose, but he's never been of interest to me. None of the lads in the village ever have been.

Monday, 26 April 1784

Suzanne came to see me at home today. Took me by surprise and no mistake! Pa was finishing up in the forge for lunch and he agreed she could join us, so I set an extra place at the table.

Suzanne was just the perfect company too. It's been just Pa and me for so long, and it did warm my heart so to see the beginnings of a smile on Pa's face when she spoke to him. She spoke of Lucy and her obvious affection for James. He's properly courting her, it seems, so there'll be no more tea parties at the inn for a while, I wouldn't have thought.

After lunch, Pa returned to the forge and Suzanne helped me tidy the pots away. She said she had wanted to spend some time alone with me. She is a much quieter girl than Lucy, and I like that. She told me that she wanted us to be close friends. It sounded so lovely to my ears for her to say that, and I could do nothing but smile!

Chapter Six

Despite the alcohol in her system, Emma couldn't sleep. All was not quite well with Lily either; she had paced up and down the bed for a little while, before jumping off and continuing on the hardwood floor, her little claws clattering like miniature stilettos in the darkness.

Emma got up to open the bedroom door, in case a feeling of being trapped was the cause of the Lily's unease. But the pacing continued. Emma went back to bed and the cat followed. There was no curling up quietly, though. Instead Lily sat bolt upright, her almond eyes wider than ever and her fur raised at the back of her fluffy neck. Her tail swished from side to side. Emma sighed. There was no way she would get to sleep while Lily was so disturbed.

A cold breeze blew through the room and Lily uttered a low growl. Emma couldn't remember leaving any of the windows open. She sat up and shivered, aware that her own hair was also standing to attention. Memories of a physics lesson involving a device that made her hair almost reach the classroom ceiling entered and then left her mind. Yes, it definitely felt like a kind of energy.

She was about to turn on the bedside light when she thought she heard a whisper and froze. In the darkness she could make out little more than the outline of the cat, now at the foot of the bed and staring at the windowsill. The deep feline growl continued.

"What is it, Lily?"

The sound of her own whisper almost scared her to death. Emma had hoped it would put the cat at ease, but no such luck.

"Oh, don't be ridiculous, Lily!" she said out loud, as much to break her own fear as the cat's. "There's nothing here. Go to sleep." And with that, she tucked herself up underneath the duvet and got comfortable.

Again, the hint of a whisper broke the silence. Emma tried to listen for words but she decided it was just a breeze rustling the leaves on the trees.

Without warning, one of her deepest erotic fantasies crept into her mind. She couldn't believe the thought would hit her at such a time, but she figured if it took her mind off the current situation enough, it may just help her get to sleep, so she closed her eyes and allowed her mind to wander, and her hand did the same.

Reaching between her legs, she found a considerable wetness had already gathered and she proceeded to stroke herself. She became aroused more quickly than usual and a moan escaped her lips. The room seemed warmer now, and Lily was beginning to settle down. Emma relaxed and her arousal soared.

She had never felt so turned on while alone before. She wondered if it was because of the tension that had been in the room. Throwing back the covers and abandoning herself to the moment, she exposed her nakedness, panting and breathless.

Oh, how good this felt! The stroking was firmer now and the intensity rose another notch. The rise and fall of her chest as heavy gasps of air flowed in and out seemed to be fuelled by an energy different from her own. This was a new power. Her skin came to life, almost as though a lover was attending to her with the lightest of touches.

A film of perspiration covered her body as the climax washed over her, the sensation more intense than she had ever experienced. Tears formed in her eyes in the afterglow, the flood of emotion almost overwhelming her.

As she lay there, recovering her breathing, Emma thought she could almost make out another whisper, or perhaps a sigh, but she was drifting into a deep and dreamless sleep now.

***

When she woke the following morning, the first thing Emma was aware of was some kind of floral scent. As she came to, she realised it was lily of the valley again, and she flashed open her eyes. Instantly, the aroma disappeared.

Lily stirred and yawned, proudly displaying a full set of healthy feline teeth. One slow blink later and it had been decided that, yes, it was definitely breakfast time, so she stood and completed a full-body stretch before leaping off the bed and staring back at Emma with a soft meow.

Seeing the cat so relaxed brought Emma great comfort. She wondered how much of last night's events she had imagined. Trying to piece things together proved futile, and her mind remained somewhat muddled after her deep sleep. It was difficult to remain focused.

One thing pleased Emma though: she had no sign of a hangover. Masturbation seemed to cure it, clearly. It had been the most intense orgasm of her life, enhanced by the feeling that she was perhaps not alone, that if she had opened her eyes, she would have found someone gazing down at her. But who? She pushed the thought from her mind. Country living was supposed to help her recover from heartbreak, not make her lose her mind.

The fact remained, however, that it was many months since she had felt the touch of a man, partly because of her marriage break-up and partly because of uncertainty about her fantasies. More and more, she had caught herself admiring other women in a way that she hadn't been brave enough to do before. Her divorce had given her an opportunity to explore this aspect of her sexuality but a chance to take it further had not yet presented itself.

A nagging ache deep in her belly reminded her of the time of the month and she rushed to the bathroom. So *that* was why the orgasm had been so intense! Satisfied by a reasonable and intelligent explanation for the evening's events, Emma continued about her day.

Now and then, though, she allowed herself a moment or two to wonder about the pungent fragrance. It wasn't a perfume she had ever owned herself.

Chapter Seven

The remainder of the day passed without event. Emma had made a point of opening all the curtains, allowing early summer warmth and light into the property.

Several times during the day, she stood in her pyjamas on the steps at the back of the house, watching a couple of sparrows playing in the stone birdbath. They splashed around and seemed to be having fun. It brought a smile to her face, as did the sun that shone generously down on the village.

For the first time in a good long while she also began to smile inwardly. The house move appeared to be working wonders for her soul, and at long last she felt she could begin her journey back to happiness.

Emma finished the filing and shredding and decided it was high time Lily had a chance to investigate her new territory. She slipped on a pair of trainers and called Lily to the back door with the keys in her hand. The cat trotted towards her with a perpendicular tail showing her excitement, until she stared into the garden and growled. A large solitary magpie was relentlessly pecking away at a patch of earth.

Emma refrained from opening the door. He was a big bird and if he was angry he might go for the cat. It wasn't unheard of. She continued to watch with interest.

Peck! Peck! Peck!

Something must have caught his eye and he wasn't giving up. Furiously, he agitated the soil. Lily grew bored and decided to stroll back to the soft cushions on the sofa, but Emma was fascinated by the bird.

Eventually her curiosity got the better of her and she unlocked the door and shooed away the bird. His fear of humans was stronger than his desire for the object and he flew off, chattering at her as he settled in a nearby tree.

Emma bent down in the flowerbed to see what it was the bird had been so interested in. The early evening sunshine was just breaking into the garden and the glare almost blinded her. After brushing away the dirt, she picked up what appeared to be a gold ring with small gems set around the band. It looked old.

Lily joined her in the garden and sniffed around the rockery close to the back door.

"Look what was in the garden, Lily. What shall we do with this?"

Meow.

After a gentle wash in soapy water, the ring sparkled a little more, and Emma held it up to the sunlight for a better look. It had an unusual design, unlike anything you'd see in a modern jeweller's shop, she decided. This was more like the kind of thing found at an antique jeweller's.

She checked the clock in the kitchen and quickly called the letting agent.

"I'm sorry, no. We've not had any reports of lost property from the previous tenant, and they didn't leave a forwarding address or contact details either, I'm afraid. I suggest you just hang on to it yourself, dear."

Emma replaced the receiver and thought for a moment. It felt strange to wear a piece of jewellery without knowing its origin. She placed it on the windowsill, just in case the previous tenant made contact with the agency.

***

Emma decided on an early night with a book, a mug of cocoa, and Lily curled up by her feet at the bottom of the bed.

The night was heavy with thunderclouds, and soon Emma regretted the hot drink. She stripped naked and removed the quilt, much to Lily's disgust. With just a thin sheet to cover her, Emma was much more comfortable and was just starting to drift off to sleep when, despite the heat and humidity, a cold chill made her shiver.

Lily sat bolt upright and hissed at the bedroom door, which Emma had left open to create a draught. Her eyes still closed, Emma caught the same fragrance of lily of the valley from the night before.

The cat remained alert and Emma held her breath. Her heart raced; she could hear it pounding in her ears. Her mouth felt dry and her hands were clammy. She sat up slowly and looked towards the door.

Even in the darkness, she could make out Lily's fur standing to attention. Without a sound, the space by the door began to change in composition. The air shimmered, like ripples on water. An image began to take shape and Emma's jaw fell open. She tried to speak but failed. A scream would have been impossible. Her leg muscles tightened and locked into place. Several times she blinked, thinking it would go away, but the apparition remained.

The cat stopped growling and sat back down on the bed, keeping a watchful eye on the activity.

The anomaly materialised fully, and Emma was staring at what appeared to be the ghost of a young woman, dressed in some kind of thin, tunic-like undergarment.

The expression on her face was one of sorrow. Emma suddenly felt overwhelmed with sadness, so much so she felt she would cry at any moment. She couldn't believe what she was seeing, but her fear was almost entirely overcome by a devastating sense of sorrow.

She looked at the girl more closely. Her shoulders drooped, her stare was distant and empty, and her arms hung by her sides. Whoever this girl was, she was troubled and heartbroken. Her hair was very long and fell in an untidy plait down one side of her body, almost reaching her waist.

Emma felt her own heart beat inside her chest. Tears collected in her eyes as her emotions reached a tipping point. When she finally took a breath, it came out as a sob. Drawing on more strength than she knew she had, she took another deep breath to try to quieten her racing heartbeat. Without knowing quite why, she knew that this entity had not come to harm her. She smiled at the ghost.

As if in response, the girl moved slowly round to the side of the bed where Emma sat, her legs still outstretched and stiff. The girl reached out and pointed to the bed as if questioning. *May I sit down?* she seemed to be saying.

Emma stole a glance at Lily, who was watching carefully but was otherwise unperturbed. She took this as a good sign and nodded slowly.

The ghost sat down, turned her face to Emma and smiled back. Her features were clearer now that she was closer. Emma figured she was quite beautiful and wondered why she was so unhappy. Seeming to read Emma's thoughts, the ghost crossed her hands over her heart and sighed. The sound was unlike anything Emma had ever heard. Like a whisper that would carry on the wind for miles, a heavy but invisible mist, it echoed between her ears and she felt her heart would break too.

So someone had broken her heart. Emma knew how that felt. She remembered the day Paul moved out, taking a piece of her with him and apparently moving on to someone else while she still drowned in her tears. The ghost smiled again and placed a hand on Emma's knee.

The unexpected contact sent a burning shiver through Emma's body and she gasped, drawing her legs up to her chest and clutching them. She broke out in a sweat and her heartbeat quickened again. The girl withdrew her hand and stood up, her eyelids dropping away from Emma's fixed stare. The shimmer appeared to wane as the girl walked back towards the door and had vanished completely by the time she had returned to the place where she had first appeared.

Gradually, Emma began to relax. Lily lay against her mistress's thigh, and the house began to feel normal again. Even the floral fragrance appeared to have lifted.

It was a long time before an uneasy sleep came to Emma that night.

***

Rob sat bolt upright in bed, coming to terms with the fact that it was just a nightmare and he had to get it out of his head.

A glance at the bedside clock told him it was a little after 4 a.m. He would have to be up in an hour anyway to drive to the site in Fosbury and it was a good three-hour journey if the traffic wasn't too bad.

Still the image haunted him. Of course, they had had to stop work and call the police straight away. The coroner was called to investigate and remove the remains. It was a full day lost, at a time when the council had already been breathing down his neck over the schedule falling behind.

Beside him, his wife stirred. "S'up?" she drawled sleepily.

Rob sighed and peeked at his erection, which was springing to life in his boxer shorts. He had half a mind to reach over and see if he couldn't seduce Selena, then thought better of it. The last time he tried that, he got thumped for his troubles. The counsellor had told them it was normal under the circumstances, especially for the woman, but it didn't do a great deal for his naturally high libido.

He decided to get up to avoid disturbing Selena any further.

"It's okay. I'm getting up."

He shoved his feet into his threadbare slippers and drew the duvet gently back over his wife's dozing form.

Downstairs in the kitchen, the coffee machine rumbled away and Rob let the dog out the back for a pee. The sky was a dark, velvety blue at this time of day, just dawning. He wanted to be on the road before the worst of the traffic got going. Throwing the espresso down his neck, he made for the bathroom.

Chapter Eight

After tossing and turning for what felt like hours, Emma became aware of the dawn chorus announcing the start of a brand new day, one for which she wasn't entirely sure she was prepared.

As she lay in bed, she recalled aspects of the previous night. Was it all a dream? she wondered, as she dragged herself out of bed and padded into the bathroom. When she came back, she stopped dead in her tracks. The ring she had discovered the day before, which she had carefully left on the kitchen windowsill, was now sitting next to the old perfume bottle on the table in the landing.

Emma froze. She was pretty confident she hadn't put it there herself, which left two options: either Lily had moved it or the ghost had. Emma looked at the cat curling around her ankles.

"Lily, have you been playing with that ring?"

Meow.

Highly unlikely, Emma thought. In her younger days, Lily had been quite the hunter in the great outdoors, but Emma considered the fact that if the cat had chosen to play with the ring, she would more likely have hidden it underneath a piece of furniture, not placed it carefully on a table.

That left only one option. Last night was not a hallucination. She *had* seen a ghost and that ghost must have placed the ring next to the perfume bottle. It was the only explanation.

Emma picked up the bottle. It hadn't occurred to her that it was anything out of the ordinary until now.

Vintage items were so in vogue these days, she had presumed the previous tenant of the house had left it behind accidentally.

The striking emerald glass contrasted with the golden stopper.

She knew the fragrance would be there, even before she had worked the stopper free. The scent filled her nostrils and she closed her eyes for a moment, picturing the forlorn face of the ghost from the night before.

What was her story? What was she seeking? What could she do to set her to rest?

***

A Google search revealed a specialist antique jeweller in a neighbouring village. Quick as a flash, Emma had showered, dressed and fed the cat. Such was her haste, she almost forgot to tuck the ring into her pocket as she sailed out of the front door towards her car.

From the exterior, the shop appeared so poorly maintained it could collapse at any moment. Emma pushed the door only a little but it gave way easily and an old-fashioned bell tinkled merrily above her head. She felt she had stepped back in time. Jewellery sparkled at her from everywhere she looked. An Aladdin's Cave of treasure was laid out before her, apparently in no particular order. Bracelets, pendants, earrings, watches for the wrist and the pocket, and snuff boxes, some plain and some engraved, all stared back at her in a dazzling, polished array of brilliance. Emma caught her breath.

"Can I help you, madam?"

The voice came from the direction of the old cash register at the back of the shop. Emma peered but could see no one. Almost camouflaged against a backdrop of old, leather-bound volumes, a man clad in a tweed jacket emerged from the bookshelves. Despite his attire, he looked somewhat younger than she had expected. It occurred to her that he may wear the outfit because it's what the customers expect, rather than to suit his own taste.

"Oh, yes, thank you. I do hope so."

She removed the ring from her pocket and handed it over.

"I wondered if you'd be able to tell me anything about this?"

The gentleman took it delicately from her fingers and studied it through his spectacles.

"Oh, I should think so." He squinted slightly. "Is it yours?"

"Well, I found it in the garden, to be honest," Emma replied. "So, if no one claims it, then, yes, I guess it is."

Her heart beat quickly in her chest. This could be the moment of truth. She watched as he turned it over between the fingers of one hand, holding a magnifying glass to his eye with the other. Would he spot something obviously sinister about the ring? Or would it be completely benign and devoid of evidence?

"Well, it's genuine for sure," The man eventually said. "A curious little piece. Really quite unusual. You found it in your garden, did you say? Yes, well. Hmmm …"

He removed his glasses and smiled at her. She smiled back and explained her story.

"Well, well, that sounds like the blacksmith's cottage, if I remember rightly. My wife will just adore this story."

Emma was confused.

"Her family comes from your village. Some years ago, she started tracing her family tree and discovered she was descended from a family who lived in that cottage at one time. I wonder if ?"

He paused for a moment. Emma had the feeling he didn't get many customers in the shop and that he was simply enjoying her presence, perhaps to the extent that he was dragging out the visit just for the company.

"I wonder if you would be so kind as to … Oh, but of course, I haven't even introduced myself. I'm so sorry."

He held out his hand for her to shake, which she duly did, as a reflex action. He smiled broadly and she decided she liked him. No one could smile that broadly and not be open and transparent.

"My name is Anthony Delaney. I was wondering if you would allow me to hold on to this piece for a couple of days, while I allow my wife, Claire, to have a look at it. She has many documents at home which may be of use in solving the mystery of its provenance."

Emma drew a deep breath from within.

"Well, I …"

"I could write you a receipt, if that would make you feel more comfortable?" Anthony was quite insistent.

In the absence of a reason to deny the poor man, Emma agreed to allow him to take the piece away. Also, she wanted to find out more herself about this mysterious little ring. His interest had lent it even more appeal.

"Allow me." He passed her a business card, seemingly before she could change her mind.

Anthony Delaney Esq.
Dealer in Antique Jewellery & Curiosities

Emma took the card. She knew at once she could trust this man and it set her mind at rest.

"Emma McVeigh," she replied. "Pleased to meet you."

"Likewise, Emma. It's rare that I have the pleasure of solving a mystery of personal significance, so you must excuse my enthusiasm." His face was really beaming now.

As she stepped back through the front door of the shop towards her car, and back into reality, she noticed Anthony had already picked up the telephone.

Chapter Nine

Summer 1784

Thursday, 6 May

A most curious thing happened today. Pa went out to the inn after he had finished at the forge for lunch, and said there would be three of us for supper. It seemed as though his thoughts were elsewhere, and so I didn't press him further on it.

So, there I am, folding linens in the sunshine and he brings home a young Mr. Joe Thatcher to meet me. It seems they'd known each other a while too. Mr. Thatcher lives down the road in Harbury and is looking for a wife, Pa says, and I am astonished.

Lord knows, I know that Pa wants to see me married. We have had such conversations before, but to actually bring someone home for me? Well, I was most shocked. I didn't know half of what to say.

Mr. Thatcher seems a nice enough gentleman, and I was polite and courteous to him, of course, but I am of no mind to be married to him. He left directly after supper and then Pa sat me down and asks me what I think of him.

Well, I was forced to tell him that I wasn't so pleased by him trying to arrange things for me, and that I should be allowed to do this in my own way. In the end, I became quite cross and blurted out that Mama would never have done such a thing to me.

He went straight to bed in a terrible rage and I am here, sat with the candle almost gone and unable to sleep for worry. I have never argued with Pa this much before, especially not since Mama passed on. I know not what I shall do.

Monday, 17 May

Pa has been very quiet since our argument. I am sad that I have hurt him so but I do not wish to make him think I am happy for him to meddle in my affairs. How can I tell him I have no wish to marry any man?

Suzanne has been visiting more often, which has raised my spirits. She says that Pa only wants for me to be happy. He likely wants me out of the way so he doesn't have to look at me and be reminded of Mama, is what I say in return. She scolds me, then, for saying such things, but I am still angry, and so she takes my hand again, and all my woes depart, leaving me carefree and breathless in my happiness.

Lucy has been courting James a lot. Suzanne reckons they are very much in love and will be married before the year is out. I say my Lucy is not so daft but we shall see soon enough.

Saturday, 4 June

Suzanne and I have had a most pleasant day out. Pa gave me a little money and encouraged me to take her into town. She had never been to Stratford-upon-Avon, and so he said I was to make sure she saw the town. I thought that he had a mind to get us both out of his way for the day for some reason, but we gathered our bonnets and off we went.

The carriage ride was uneventful, although Suzanne felt uneasy. She had not taken many carriage rides since her parents' accident, but I sat right next to her for comfort and she took to smiling by the time we reached the town.

We took a walk along the river and found a tea room. Suzanne insisted on cream scones and then bit so hard into one she got a splodge of cream all over her nose! I gasped, as we were in such a fancy place, but then we both laughed so hard I thought we would be asked to leave the shop. But the woman behind the counter smiled on us and we stayed to finish our tea.

After our tea, we walked some more and came upon the birthplace of William Shakespeare. It's truly amazing to think that he was walking around the town just over two hundred years ago, just as Suzanne and I were walking around this afternoon.

Mama used to talk of a book she once had, with his plays inside. I remember saying to her that a play should be acted out upon a stage. What use is it inside a book? But then she would say only the rich would ever see the plays and the rest of us had to make do without. She would look wistful then, so I asked no more.

A strange and wonderful thing happened as we walked about the town. Suzanne was strolling next to me and, come to think of it, was fiddling with the ribbon of her bonnet, as if to untie it there and then. I put out my hand to stop her and, imagine my surprise when she took my hand and kissed it. My heart was beating so loudly I felt sure she must hear it. It was fit to burst right through my chest. I wonder if she had those same feelings that I did at that moment. Certainly I am the happiest girl in Fosbury tonight as I write this!

Sunday, 19 June

Suzanne and I walked in the fields again today. The weather was very warm indeed and Pa did the right thing to warn us of the strong sunshine. I remembered to bring my bonnet and to sit underneath the trees. We spent all afternoon outdoors, so long that when we saw the sun bobbing down behind the trees, we felt sure it would be late and past our suppertime. Pa was not best pleased when we came home so late, but all was forgiven when Suzanne smiled at me and said that I needed to spend more time outdoors for my complexion.

Wednesday, 6 July
Oh, it has been so long since I have written, but I could not have missed a single moment without my Suzanne.

Since that first day when she held my hand, I swear that I have been in love and now she tells me that she feels it too. What joy I have in my heart!

Just this very day, my word of honour, she kissed me on the lips, so now I know it is certain to be true!

We were out walking, as we do almost every day now, by the woodland area out in the fields behind the cottage. No one saw us together, I'm sure. We strolled down by the stream, running so full because of the recent rains. The grass was dry, though, thankfully, and we sat down on the banks and watched the water flowing in the sunshine.

Then she took my hand in hers, as she so often does nowadays. An expression crossed her face. I was worried for a moment, as she looked so serious. Was she ill, I asked?

No, she was quite fine, she said and smiled, asking me to be patient while she explained herself.

She said that she had begun to harbour a feeling more than friendship for me and that she felt embarrassed by it. That was when my heart melted and I grasped both her hands in sheer delight and admitted that I too had those same feelings and for some time.

It was at that very moment that she leaned forward and pressed her lips to mine. The world stood still, I swear. My heart pounded and I began to glow, such was the force of my passion.

She explained so much to me in that one kiss. I knew then why I had paid no interest in any of the men in the village, for I was not meant to be with any of their kind.

Poor Pa suspects nothing, of course. For shame, I do hope he never will. It would be too much for him to bear.

Friday, 22 July

Well, I'm sure my heart can take no more of this emotion or I shall go quite mad!

My beautiful Suzanne and I have now declared our love for each other, and I told her in that same instant that I had been in love with her all these past months since we first met. I am beside myself with joy, but also fearful for what the future may hold for us and I am in knots inside when I think of it.

I know not what we shall do about this. For sure, we can tell no one in the village. Unlike Lucy and James, we cannot be married. Indeed, we must not speak of it to anyone but ourselves for to do so would bring shame on both our households.

Perhaps we shall run away, but I would miss Pa so dearly and I could not leave him all alone. So, we must remain here though not live as lovers. Whatever shall we do?

Chapter Ten

Emma frowned to herself as she arrived back at the cottage. She had to return to work in another week and she didn't want anything hanging over her and clouding her judgement. There would be enough catching up to do and distractions would be unwelcome.

Lewis's face popped into her mind at that point. Now *there* was a distraction that was welcome indeed. Some relaxation in his company would be just the thing, but she didn't want to come across as too forward and send the wrong signals.

His cottage was very much like hers. Indeed, the exterior had the same local stone and thatched roof with tiny windows in the upstairs rooms.

There was shouting coming from inside the cottage. Emma almost decided to go home but, on account of the fact that she could only hear Lewis's voice, decided to stay put. She could only make out one word.

"Annabelle!"

She decided to wait until after she heard the telephone receiver being slammed down before knocking on the door.

"Hey, what have you been up to?"

Lewis looked exasperated. He opened the door just enough to let his head peep around and look at her.

"Is this a bad time? I can come back if it's awkward?"

"Not at all. But can you give me a few minutes and I'll come round to yours?"

Emma smiled. She had obviously embarrassed him, and should have gone back home after all and waited until later.

"I just wondered if you fancied another dinner. My treat this time."

"I'll be round in ten minutes when I've finished up here, if that's okay?"

***

Lewis caught his breath as he closed the door. Damn her to arrive at such an inconvenient time! No, it wasn't her fault. How could she have possibly known Annabelle would call at such a time? He cursed his ex-girlfriend. He was in no hurry to see her again, even if it was to pay him back some money. He certainly didn't need it. Well, she could bloody well wait until it was convenient for him.

Moments later, Emma was answering her own door.

Lewis looked around the hallway and kitchen briefly as Emma fetched her coat.

"I see you're making the place your own." He was looking through her collection of cookery books when she returned. "Are you really a domestic goddess or are these all for show?"

"Is that a not-so-subtle hint that you'd like me to cook for you? Careful what you wish for!"

"Doesn't have to be anything gourmet," he teased. "Oh, and I don't eat cheese, just so you know."

"That's weird! You don't eat cheese. There must be thousands of different cheeses." She looked at him quizzically.

"I like to be different. Shall we?"

He held open the door for her and they walked towards the pub, chatting with ease.

The first couple of drinks went down very easily indeed. Emma spent an hour wondering whether she should tell him about the ghost and the ring, while simultaneously trying to make small talk. Lewis saw right through her subterfuge.

"Now then, you didn't ask me here to talk that kind of rubbish all night. What's on your mind?"

She tried to look him in the eyes with confidence but her voice faltered. "Well," she started, taking a large gulp of wine before continuing in a whisper, "I think the cottage might be haunted."

There was a long pause, during which Emma felt that even Time was standing still and waiting for her to start laughing. She stared at Lewis, who took an equally large gulp from his glass, swallowed, set it down carefully on the table and took a deep breath.

This is it, she thought. He's going to tell me the stress of moving has done things to my head.

He was clearly thinking what to say.

"Aren't you going to say something?" She could bear his silence no longer.

He took another deep breath.

"It makes several things fall into place, for sure."

Now it was Emma's turn to be quiet. She hadn't expected him to believe her.

"You see, the tenant before you was quite an elderly lady. She didn't stay long, about a month, that was it. There was no notice when she moved out, apparently. I happened to spot a car from the agency that had let it out. They were trying to get hold of her. I wondered what had happened.

"Then I went to the shop to ask if they knew anything. The old lady used to visit the shop every day, you see. They said she'd told them there was this strange smell about the place. A perfume she couldn't get rid of, no matter how hard she tried."

"A perfume?" Emma stared in astonishment.

"Like flowers, she told them. Especially when the moon was around full."

As if rehearsed, they both flicked their heads towards the night sky.

"Last night, I think," Lewis said.

There was an uncomfortable silence between them for a moment.

"It's lily of the valley," Emma said.

"Sorry, what?"

"The perfume. My grandmother used to wear it. That's how I know. I've smelled it too, in the house. It's beautiful. And ..."

He took her hand in his, for reassurance, she thought. "Jeez, you're freezing cold!

"Lewis, I've seen her. I found a ring in the garden yesterday and I brought it inside to wash it. I left it by the kitchen sink, I know I did, and during the night, she came. She glowed, she was quite young but forlorn. As I watched her, I felt sad beyond belief, like she was making me feel her pain."

"You mean there's actually a ghost?"

"If you don't believe me, that's okay. I thought it was mad too, but this morning when I woke, the ring had moved next to an old perfume bottle I found when I moved in. The fragrance is the same, but it's not stale at all. It's fresh."

He squeezed her hand gently. "Let's just say I have an open mind about these things. I've had a couple of experiences myself that I can't explain."

They sat in silence for a while, Lewis still holding her hand. Emma was relieved that he hadn't laughed at her. But having said it all aloud, she was giving it credibility in her own mind. She couldn't pretend it wasn't happening any more, now that she'd told someone.

"Well, sitting here thinking about it isn't going to help. Let's change the subject," said Lewis.

The barman was calling time before she knew it. Lewis had made good on his suggestion. They had discussed everything from music and film to sport, current affairs and a whole host of things besides. Emma had laughed until tears poured down her cheeks, and argued until the same cheeks blazed with fury. She drained the rest of her glass. She swayed a little as she stood to put on her coat.

"I think, madam, you should probably not be alone tonight, the amount you've had to drink. I have a spare room at mine, you know, in case you don't want to go home tonight, after what we talked about earlier."

Emma grasped his hand and squeezed. It felt comfortable.

"That would be lovely."

She grinned up at him. He really was rather lovely after all. He took her by the hand and led her out of the pub and all the way to his house. She wasn't at all phased when, after closing the door behind them, he moved in to kiss her, nor did she so much as flinch when, while standing in his kitchen, his tongue entered her mouth, circling and caressing hers as she moaned in return.

She didn't feel at all surprised when he started to remove her clothes, nibbling gently as he gradually exposed areas of flesh until she stood naked.

No, it all felt so natural and so perfectly expected that once he had undressed himself, he should take her up to bed and caress, lick and stroke every inch of her, bringing her to climax again and again, before entering her to find his own release.

***

Back at the blacksmith's cottage, Lily was asleep on the sofa, no doubt dreaming about catching mice. Upstairs, an almost full moon shone down onto an empty bed.

Chapter Eleven

Dawn broke later than usual the following morning, owing to the dreadful weather. Emma lay awake next to the sleeping Lewis, replaying the previous night's drunken fumble over and over in her mind. How could she have allowed this to happen?

There was only one thing to be done. She rose carefully to avoid waking him, scribbled a short note and left.

The cloud cover seemed appropriate as she hung her head in shame on the walk back home. She wasn't sure that even the heavy rain could wash away her iniquity.

The expression on the cat's face spoke volumes. Her mistress had not been home for night-time cuddles and was also late with breakfast.

Full of apologies, Emma set about rectifying her appalling standard of service, then slumped onto the sofa with a deep sigh. She switched her phone off. A call from Lewis would be unwelcome. She wouldn't have been able to think of what to say to him anyway.

She briefly entertained the idea that she may have ruined her only friendship in the village, but decided that the middle of a hangover was not the best time to consider such things. Instead, she trudged back through to the kitchen and boiled the kettle for a large mug of hot chocolate, her comfort in times of distress.

Heaving herself upstairs, she ran a bath and shrugged off yesterday's clothes. She stank of a heady combination of stale perfume and sex.

She caught a glimpse of her naked form in the bathroom mirror, then wished she hadn't. It had been many years since she had been what her mother would call slim and, although not very overweight, there were plenty of lumps and bumps that she would rather weren't there.

Her gaze was distracted by something on the landing table, next to the vintage perfume bottle. She spun round to see it properly and gasped. A single stem of drooping, bell-shaped white flowers was sat upon a small handkerchief. Lily of the valley.

Surely Lewis wasn't playing a trick on her? He wouldn't have had time to jump out of bed and sprint to her house. Besides, he had no key and there were no signs of forced entry.

After her bath, Emma put the stem in the only vase she could find and placed it on her dressing table, facing the window and overlooking the garden and woodland at the back of the cottage. She was still deep in thought when the landline rang, making her jump.

"Miss McVeigh, thank goodness! I called your mobile but it went straight to voicemail."

"Oh hi, Anthony."

"I have some wonderful news about your ring. You remember I said I would speak with my wife, Claire? Well, she's found out some very interesting things and, well, rather than discuss them in the shop, she suggested that I invite you round for tea at our house this afternoon. Say about 4 o'clock-ish?"

Predicting that her hangover would have sufficiently subsided by then, Emma agreed and replaced the receiver. It would be a perfect way to take her mind off the situation with Lewis.

The rain had stopped by the middle of the afternoon, but the clouds continued to threaten, and there was more forecast for the evening. The view from the doorstep of Anthony and Claire's stretched out across a deep valley and it seemed the bad weather was coming in from that direction. The door opened behind Emma just as she shivered from the damp.

"Oh, do come in out of that weather!" Anthony exclaimed, taking her coat and hanging it on the stand in the hallway. "The living room is just through here."

The interior of the house was much like the jewellery shop in the apparently haphazard arrangement of books and ornaments. The shelves were overflowing with all kinds of volumes, old and new. Emma saw books on local history and jewellery from different periods in history, as well as an assortment of travel guides.

"We like to visit a new country every time we go on holiday," said Anthony. "Here's your ring. I'll go and fetch Claire. She's very excited."

He presented Emma with the ring in a small box. When she opened it, the sparkle almost took her breath away. He had polished it beyond recognition, and it shone in stark contrast to the small piece of black velvet cloth on which it now sat.

Emma plonked herself on the sofa and removed the ring from the box. It was hovering over the tip of her fingernail as she was about to try it on when there was a voice behind her.

"Before you do that, dear, you might want to know a little more about it."

Claire Delaney was an attractive, homely lady. She brought a tray with tea, biscuits and cake and smiled broadly at Emma. "It's lovely to meet you," she said. She sat down next to Emma and picked up a large folder from the coffee table.

"I started tracing my family history several years ago, when I was put in charge of local history at the library," she explained. "And, I'm very glad I did, because my mother died only a year later, so I was able to share with her some of the information I had learned before she passed away."

"Oh, I'm sorry," Emma said.

"Don't be. She had been ill for some time and it was something of a relief in the end. So, this is your house, yes?"

Emma peered at the old black and white photo depicting a youngish couple, frowning. The steps and front door were unmistakable.

"This photo was taken around 1912," Claire said. "It's my mother's parents a year after they were married. It was their first house, and where my mother grew up.

"My father wasn't a blacksmith, but my grandmother's older brother was. Unfortunately, he died in a tragic accident at the forge up the road. He was already widowed and without children, so his sister inherited the cottage. Perhaps that's why they don't look terribly happy in the photo."

"Oh, how sad." Emma looked at the photo again.

"Going back further, there had been black- and whitesmiths in the family for generations. Census records helped me for some time, but they weren't really useful until about 1841, which was when names were required to be recorded for the first time. Anyway, you're probably wondering what all this has to do with your ring."

As if to prolong the anticipation, Claire poured the tea.

"I remember my grandmother saying they found a ring at the house shortly after they moved in. Turned out it was some kind of family heirloom, been around for several generations. It was only worn once though, apparently. No one ever discovered why."

"So," Anthony chipped in, "we both did some sleuthing. As I said to you in the shop the other day, it's an unusual piece. After I polished it, I was surprised that it appears not to have been worn much, if at all. A hallmark can be seen, which dates it to around the late eighteenth century. It was marked at the assay office in Birmingham. I can also tell you it's actually gold-plated but not with the skill you would expect of a master jeweller. I think this is crafted by someone who was still learning their trade. Perhaps even an apprentice whitesmith."

Claire's eyes shone as she took up the story, and Emma listened in silence, hanging on her every word. "The style is very much of that period but, as Anthony said, this piece is likely to have been made for sentimental reasons, as opposed to commercial ones. It was fashioned out of love for someone. The gemstones are garnets, quite fashionable at the time, and widely available within the trade. They are said to represent constancy and loyalty. These days you might see them in friendship rings, but back then they might have been used in an engagement ring for those for whom diamonds were too expensive.

"Which brings me back to my research. Before my mother died, she told me of an old family story that she had heard from her grandmother. It involved some scandal of a young woman who hanged herself in the forge. Something about a lover. Her name was Grace, apparently, although I can find no record of her."

A shiver ran up the length of Emma's spine at the sound of the name and she felt faint. She was speechless.

***

Crooked fingers. No, not crooked. More like spindly. No, wrong again. Bones. That's what they were. No flesh or muscle. Just bones.

Attached to them are the twisted radius and ulna and the lower humerus is visible beneath the tattered sleeve of an old nightgown of some sort. The fabric is yellowing and frayed at the edges. It's been eaten away where moths have nibbled away at it over the years.

Rob pays more attention to this than he would normally, to delay the inevitable moment when he must meet the fiendish gaze of this monster. But do so he must.

The skull sits at a horrific angle, cocked to one side, about to fall off, it seems. A maniacal laugh echoes all around as the bony digits reach out, closing around his neck.

Rob sat up in bed, panting. It had been many years since he'd had such a vivid nightmare.

Dawn was breaking through the thin curtains of the rented room so he figured he'd best get up. He shuffled to the bathroom and stared in the small shaving mirror. He tried his best to gel his hair just the way he liked it but it wasn't playing the game this morning. Fuck it. There was a lot to catch up on today, now they had the site to themselves once again.

Chapter Twelve

The patter of rain on the window brought Lewis to his senses. For some reason he couldn't quite explain, he knew even before he opened his eyes that Emma had already left, but he turned his head for a glimpse nonetheless.

He reached under the covers to the empty side of the bed. Cold. She had left a while ago, then. He sighed, then spotted the note on the bedside table.

> *Morning,*
> *Sorry I had to dash.*
> *Em.*

No kiss. Was that significant? Perhaps. He wasn't sure if his headache was as a result of the over-indulgence the previous night or of his thinking about the current situation. He rose to make a coffee and decided it was definitely the former.

He knew he shouldn't have slept with her. He really hoped he hadn't screwed up a friendship with her, or a very promising anything else for that matter.

As the kettle boiled, he stared out at his sodden garden. This weather had better clear up. All the jobs he had lined up at the moment were outdoors and he hated gardening in the rain. He also needed not to get too involved with Emma. He couldn't risk all that hurt all over again. And from what she had told him, neither could she.

He recalled the softness of her naked body against his as he kissed and caressed her, feeling her body wrap itself around him as he entered her. It had all felt so right, so natural, so … Uncomplicated. He wasn't used to that. So many girls from his past had proved to be high maintenance and emotionally needy. Despite her recent break-up and the obvious heartbreak, Emma was a breath of fresh air.

He took a quick shower to clear his head. A day's work would sort him out, no doubt. A drop of rain would likely do him the world of good, especially if the landlady at The White Horse gave him a free lunch again.

He threw on a tatty old pair of jeans and made his way back to the pub.

"Morning, Lewis!"

Gwen always looked so chipper, he thought to himself.

"Morning. I was wondering if now would be a good time to finish off the job I started round the back, if Pete was about?"

"Well, actually, love, he's not up yet." Gwen tossed her bottle-blonde hair over her shoulder and giggled. "It was rather a late one last night, you see. Speaking of which, I saw you with your lady friend. Is this a girlfriend at last?"

"Oh, err …" He wasn't prepared for questions about Emma just yet. Too awkward. "She's new to the village, so I'm just showing her around really, you know."

"Well, you seemed to be getting on famously over dinner. I was sneaking a peek from the kitchen now and then. Sorry, I couldn't resist." She winked at him and

Lewis tried to hide his discomfort. "I see you left before the bar closed as well. Not like you."

Her intonation seemed to beg an answer but he refused to engage with her banter. Gwen had flirted with him ever since the first time he walked in the pub when he moved to the village, and she made no secret of it in front of her husband either, which Lewis thought distinctly sluttish.

"Well, I'll go and see what Pete's up to," she said, turning on her leopard print heels and running up the stairs.

Lewis shook his head. Gwen had a good heart, but she wasn't the sharpest tool in the box.

A cough from the corner of the pub startled him. He whipped his head round to see a man choking on a piece of toast.

"My fault," the guy said, after Lewis slapped him on the back. "I was just thinking how she seems to flirt with every man and gossip about every woman. Thank you." He coughed for the last time and appeared to regain his composure.

"You're welcome. Sorry if I disturbed your breakfast," Lewis said.

"Oh, not at all. I'm done anyway. Gotta get to work."

He took a large gulp of coffee and let out a satisfied belch.

"I've seen you in here before, I think. Perhaps you'll let me buy you a drink later. You know, for not letting me choke to death."

"Thanks. Yeah, that'd be great. I'll be in here."

"Rob Thornton. I'm the site manager over at Fosse Rise, the new development." His handshake wasn't as firm as Lewis expected.

"Lewis Carrington. Good to meet you, Rob. I won't keep you if you want to get off."

"Sure, yeah, well, I'll see you later then."

He grabbed his newspaper and shouted his thanks up the stairs before hurrying out into the overcast morning.

Pete came tumbling down the stairs, rolling a T-shirt over his large beer gut, only just restrained by an optimistically-sized pair of jeans.

"Lewis! Perfect day for it, mate. I've got some debris needs shifting into the skip out back if that's OK? Gardening can be done when the weather's better, eh? I wanna get the function room finished before the summer kicks off in earnest. You all right for fetching and carrying today?"

"Sure, no problems," Lewis replied. "Just point me in the general direction."

***

The rain had stopped but the heavy clouds meant that the humidity was high and the threat of further downpours was never far away.

Lewis stopped for a moment and mopped the sweat from his brow. How had his life come to this?

A painful memory resurfaced in his head. Annabelle, horizontal with her legs in the air, her skirt hitched up and around her waist and his father fucking her on his large, imposing leather-bound desk.

Acidic spittle gathered in his throat and he spat it out onto the ground. Whore! She had been broke when he persuaded his father to take her on as his PA. Freshly arrived into the UK from South Carolina, she needed a job to support her silicone-implants and cocktail-fuelled lifestyle and she found the Carrington family just to her liking. She and Lewis started dating in a matter of days, but Lewis didn't have the head for business that his father expected and Annabelle clicked that his future was uncertain. It was the senior Carrington she really wanted; that was where the money lay.

Having said that, he had wondered why the previous assistant had left in such a hurry. Now he knew. His father had never cared about either him or his poor mother. As far as he knew, neither his father nor his spiteful sister Catherine ever visited Mrs. Carrington. It was just as well. She didn't know what was going on half the time and she needed calm and collected people around her. Lewis knew just how to sit with her, hold her hand and tell her stories. She would have wanted him to settle down with someone better than Annabelle. Despite her mental state, she would still have seen straight through her, he was certain.

Without warning, Emma's face sprang to mind again. Now there was someone who was utterly grounded. She had her own share of problems, sure, but she wasn't pretentious like Annabelle. She wasn't expecting her Prince Charming to turn up with a fat bank balance and an expensive sports car. She wasn't even looking for a Prince Charming right now.

A pang of regret stabbed his heart; she was emotionally vulnerable right now. He had allowed his sex drive to get the better of him while under the influence of alcohol. Hopefully, she wouldn't hold it against him. She wasn't exactly innocent though. Those beautiful sad eyes and her sensitivity were all part of her charm, and once he started taking off her clothes, she had just melted into him.

"Maybe I should paint Emma," he said out loud, then shook his head and snorted. As if. After what happened last night, she probably wouldn't want to see him again.

Chapter Thirteen

It was well after dark when Emma returned home. The moon was shining into the bedroom when Emma reached the top of the stairs. The single stem remained in the vase and she carefully placed the ring next to it on the table. She undressed quietly and got into bed, naked as a baby. The rain had done nothing to kill the summer balminess; it was to be another humid night.

The soft lunar rays brought her comfort as she lay under a single sheet. Her thoughts turned to the revelations she had heard at Anthony and Claire's house.

Grace.

Again, Emma shivered at the name. There was something about it that made her uneasy. Was that the name of her ghost? What had happened to her?

Almost before the questions had formed in her head, a faint scent filled the room and she felt herself drift into a dreamlike state.

Another shiver woke her, some time later; the scent was stronger now. How long had she been asleep? She refrained from opening her eyes but, in truth, she knew what she would see when she opened them.

The shimmering apparition was less opaque this time, although some transparency remained. The forlorn expression was gone too, replaced by bright, smiling eyes; this time, the ghost looked happy and vibrant. She wore the same shift, but this time it was completely open at the front, right to the waist. It swung open as she moved towards the bed, to reveal ample breasts, to which the phantom paid no heed whatsoever.

Emma was much less fearful this time, though she couldn't think why. She sat up to get a better look. This girl did not mean to harm her, but she did seem to want to be near her. Emma stared open-mouthed at the girl's breasts, then back at her face. There was something else going on too. She began to feel aroused. And she liked it.

Despite the chill in the room, Emma felt hot. Perspiration began to accumulate on her back and between her legs. Her breath quickened and she became aware of her own bosom heaving as she breathed deeper and deeper. It almost came as a relief when the ghost placed a hand upon hers, as if asking to sit on the bed. Emma expected the touch to be cold, but the skin was warm, like a living human being.

"Grace?" Her whisper cut the air like a sliver of glass.

Her visitor nodded slightly then held a finger to her lips, requesting silence as she shuffled up the bed right next to where Emma sat. The urge to pull her knees up to her chest was overwhelming, but Emma resisted. All she could think about was how it would feel to kiss this beautiful girl, this glowing, slightly transparent figure sitting next to her on the bed.

As if the girl had read her thoughts, she leaned in closer, almost touching her face and then paused, as though gauging Emma's reaction. Emma nodded a little, hoping to be understood.

There was no holding back then. Lips touched lips, gently at first, then more forceful. There was a yearning in this kiss; Emma could feel it. She briefly wondered whether the ghost had kissed many other girls, or whether she had waited all this time for someone who would be receptive. Maybe that was why the previous tenants had not stayed at the cottage for long – they had been frightened of her.

Emma felt a hand on her waist and opened her eyes just as the kiss broke off. The second hand reached up and stroked her face. She stared into the eyes of the girl and saw pure unadulterated lust. She was breathless with intoxication.

Emma had often wondered what it would be like to kiss a girl. Never in her wildest fantasies had she ever thought it would be quite like this.

She lifted her hand and placed it on the ghost's arm, stroking it. It felt just like another woman.

Grace. I can call her that now, Emma thought, after what we have just shared.

As she watched her hand stroking, her eyes drifted upwards towards the shimmering face to find it was no longer transparent at all. Sat beside her now was a figure that was to all intents and purposes a living, breathing human being. The bewildered expression on her face drew a smile from Grace and just the slightest whisper: "You see with your emotion, Emma. Your desire feeds me."

The stroking became stronger, and Emma's hand rose up Grace's arm, catching the edge of the shift and sliding underneath towards her shoulder. Grace pulled back a little. Had she gone too far?

She stood and, in one swift movement, pulled the shift over her head and threw it onto the floor in a heap.

Emma gasped at her beauty. How many people have ever seen a naked ghost, she wondered? Grace turned back the sheet that covered Emma and sat back down. Her gaze was appraising but not judgemental. A finger traced a line from her lips down her chin and neck, between her breasts and down her stomach. Then it paused, before gliding softly between her legs.

Emma's heart thundered with anticipation. There was an ache deep within her and she longed to open her legs and reveal the wetness she knew would have gathered. The kissing resumed, more passionate this time, and Emma reached out to touch the breasts she had been staring at for some moments.

Grace moved across the bed to lie next to her, keeping a hand between Emma's legs and teasing them further apart. Her carefully placed fingers seemed to know every inch of her, reaching exactly the right spot. Emma was moaning and writhing in the sweet bliss of arousal. Her climax washed over her, bringing release and a sense of calm and peace.

When she opened her eyes, Grace was holding out a finger for her to taste. She licked slowly, savouring her own muskiness. It seemed a natural next step to reach out towards Grace and slide her hand down between her legs. The first sensation was of heat; the second was the soft hair, which parted easily to reveal the moist inner lips.

Emma looked up into Grace's face, about to apologise for her clumsiness, but Grace put a finger to her lips and then said, "Do what you feel." The whisper was barely audible, and her head tipped back in ecstasy.

It seemed Emma was doing the right thing. Grace was squirming around, her chest heaving as if breathless in the throes of passion. Her body twisted and contorted, hips bucking wildly, but Emma continued stroking. Grace held still for a moment then, and a breathless sigh escaped her lips. She relaxed in a heap and gazed longingly up at Emma.

Neither said anything for a few moments, but remained bathed in the light of the moon, which was dropping in the sky behind the trees. Grace leaned over and cradled Emma's face in her hands. In the moonlight, Emma thought she could make out tears glistening in Grace's eyes and a satisfied smile.

The kiss this time held an emotional connection. There was passion, but the overriding emotion was gratitude. They held hands for a while, staring into each other's souls, until Emma found the most peaceful and restful sleep she had had in some time.

Chapter Fourteen

Autumn/winter 1784

Sunday, 5 September
*The most beautiful ring I ever saw sits in a box in Pa's room.
Or at least it used to until today. Pa told me some years ago
of its existence. He made it for Mama, but she died before it
was finished, so she never wore it. He has kept it there until
now.*

*So it sprang to my mind just the other day that it would
make a perfect gift for my Suzanne, and she could wear it as a
token of my affection.*

*She was a little nervous at first, but when I told her she
could wear it on her right hand instead, she smiled and told
me she would be proud to have it. I was never so happy as
when I placed it on her finger. I know we can never be
married but her acceptance of Mama's ring is good enough for
me to feel that we are forever in each other's hearts..*

Thursday, 9 September
*Today I feel so dreadful. Suzanne has hurt me more than I
have the words to describe.*

*We were sat over in the fields again, in the shade of our
favourite tree, and she started talking about Lucy's
forthcoming wedding to James and how she will be looked
after for the rest of her days.*

*I can see why she worries about such things. Her being
orphaned and such, she has no parents to support her. But I
had a mind that she could move into our home, with Pa and*

me. I know he will have a little money set aside for me, the way he goes on about marriage.

But no, she says she is adamant that she wants a husband and that our love cannot endure. A child's play is what she called it, and it hurt me to the core. I was stunned, I was, sitting there and staring at her. She knows the way I think about men, that I could never be with a man. I thought she was the same way, too.

She says she loves me but she wants to have a life with means, and of course, that means a man. Truly, I am not that concerned with means, and we would be happy, I know we would, but she will have none of it. I know Pa would provide for all of us, if necessary. But if it's not what she wants, then I cannot help her.

Truly, I do not know what I am to do.

Monday, 4 October

Pa has taken on a new apprentice today. His name is Tom. He looked at me in a certain way, though, which made me feel uneasy. I do hope he's not got anything improper on his mind. I don't want anything of that, not with him.

I wonder sometimes if there's something wrong with me. Lucy is still chattering on about James. I am sick to death of it. But, for me, I've never felt anything like she does for any of the boys. Pa often asks me if there is anyone I like, but in all sincerity, I cannot tell him that a single boy shines out from the rest.

Poor, dear Pa. He loves me so, I know. I do wish he'd leave me be.

Wednesday, 24 November

Pa has been off to the inn again this afternoon. I am unhappy that he is neglecting the forge. Young Tom has not been started long, and is perhaps not confident enough that he can take on so much just yet.

I do hope Father has not turned to drink. I smell nothing on his clothes or breath, only that stale tobacco used by some of the men who drink there. I wonder to myself why he should spend so much time there if he does not drink. What can there be to do?

Suzanne was not at home when I called upon her yesterday. I want to make up for what happened between us the other week. I feel sure I can persuade her to continue our affair, and that no man will ever make her so happy, not like I can. Surely she can see that.

Wednesday, 1 December

Words cannot express the loneliness I feel at this moment. I am utterly undone and I know of no way this situation can be resolved.

My beautiful, smiling Suzanne is to be married to none other than my own Pa. I have been betrayed by them both, and I am left with no soul in whom to confide my feelings.

There I was, preparing a supper for Pa and me, when he walked into the cottage with her on his arm. It seems he has had her in mind for some considerable time since. But of course how could he have known of us? Suzanne has asked me never to speak a word of our love, to swear on my life that we were always just friends.

But what sort of life shall I have now? My sweetheart, my Pa and I, all living under the same roof, but with them being married to one another? I cannot bear it, and I will not!

71

Whatever is to become of me?

I shall never love another. My heart belongs to one, and one alone. For sure, I shall die an old maid or I shall die from grief.

Saturday, 5 December

It is to be on Friday in two weeks' time, this wedding.

I am trying so hard to keep my feelings hidden from Pa. I think him contented. He has asked me to press his Sunday shirt on Thursday evening, in good time for his big day.

I feel as though to do so would be to help him into this marriage and I fear I cannot do it.

Suzanne has spoken with me.

She does not love him, I know it! She told me as much herself.

I hope Mama cannot look down upon us from heaven above and see what Pa is doing. I know he wants a companion, but he does not need my Suzanne for that. For sure, what else am I here for, but to keep him company?

Tuesday, 14 December

I saw Lucy today. She can see my despair but I dare not tell her the cause. The entire village would know in no time at all, and I could not shame Pa so.

She tried in vain to coax a smile from my face but I stared back at her.

"Your eyes are empty, Grace," she said. "Why must you be so sad when your Pa is so happy?"

I know not how long this melancholy will continue. Perhaps it will be always. Pa talks of gathering holly branches for decorating the cottage door this year. I am in no mood for Christmas.

I cannot think beyond the end of each day, wishing it were my last.

Chapter Fifteen

Emma's eyelids fluttered in the glare of the morning sunlight, which shone through the open curtains and bathed her in a glow of vitality. It could all have been a dream but for the slight indentation in the bed next to her and the fresh stem of lily of the valley flowers on the pillow. The events of the night before played over and over in her mind until nothing but confusion reigned.

Without a second thought, she picked up her phone and dialled the only person she knew who could be of any help.

"Darling! How *are* you? How's the new house?"

Emma rarely saw Meredith these days. It was a far cry from their university days, propping up some bar or other almost every night.

"Well, I'm good, thanks. And the house is lovely, but that's kind of why I'm calling. I could really do with some help. It's, err … well, it's haunted."

"Oh, wow! Fantastic! okay, what's been happening?"

Emma sat up in bed and organised her thoughts.

"It starts with a chill in the air and then there's a smell, like perfume."

"What does it smell like?" She could hear Meredith scribbling notes at the other end of the line.

"Lily of the valley. I'd know it anywhere. A sprig of the flowers was left as well. I think the fragrance is linked to an old perfume bottle that was here when I moved in. I polished it and put it on the table in the hall upstairs because it's pretty. Oh, and I found a ring, too. It seems to have been hers."

Meredith's voice quickened at the other end of the line. She was clearly very excited. "Oh, you have awoken something, I think. It may have been a personal tie to the spirit and it's tying you to her. I'm presuming it's a woman, with a scent like that. Have you seen anything?"

"Oh, it's better than that. Yes, I've seen her. The first time she looked sad and forlorn. I was terrified. But then, last night …" Emma took a deep breath. Meredith was a very open-minded person, but a tiny flicker of doubt in Emma's mind was refusing to extinguish itself.

"Yes, go on …"

"Well, she came into the room and, Meredith, I don't know how to say this. You're the only person I can tell. She seduced me."

There was a sharp intake of breath down the phone. "Right, sit tight. I'm coming straight over. Give me a couple of hours."

***

The cute little MG sports car pulled up on the road at the bottom of the steps. Yet another summer shower had just passed overhead, and as Emma opened the door to welcome her friend, the raindrops sparkled like jewels on the rockery flowers.

"Wow, what a charming little place, Darling! Just the perfect little hideaway for you right now."

Meredith was wearing one of her "spiritual" outfits. The heavy crushed velvet seemed out of place for the season, but it suited her perfectly as she sashayed through the front door. "Oh, yes," she said, as Emma

75

closed the door behind her, "I can feel sadness here. Yes, we have some work to do to free this poor soul. Anyway, be a love and put the kettle on while I set up. Then you can tell me all about your lesbian romp, you crazy minx."

Emma heaved a sigh of relief. Meredith had such confidence. She was a woman who had a solution for everything, regardless of the problem. Sometimes, it would be unconventional, but as long as there was tea involved, nothing seemed insurmountable.

When she returned to the living room with steaming mugs, Emma could see her coffee table had been transformed into a kind of altar with a single lit candle placed on top of a black cloth, printed in the centre of which was a pentagram. Small pieces of paper sat in a row on the cloth, labelled "Yes", "No", "Maybe" and "Not Advisable".

"So, you still do all this spiritual stuff?" Emma asked.

"Oh yes, honey. It's proved invaluable in helping people. Now then, do you have an object I can use? That ring you found, perhaps? Oh, and bring the perfume bottle too, just in case."

Meredith sat cross-legged and barefoot in front of the table and took a chain from a small velvet drawstring purse strapped to her waist. Hanging from the chain was a large polished crystal in a vibrant shade of purple, held in a three-pointed clasp at the top.

"I'm going to do a pendulum ritual," Meredith declared. "It's gentler than using a Ouija board and should keep away undesirable spirits. We want to talk to *your* spirit, not just anyone who wants to join in the fun."

Emma knelt opposite her friend. She took a deep breath to try and calm her racing heart, but it proved futile. Until lately, she had been sceptical about the existence of the supernatural, but then she had met the beautiful Grace, and now she believed anything was possible.

"We're going to ask a series of questions, the answers to which are written on the pieces of paper. The direction in which the pendulum swings will give us the answer. You ready?"

Emma nodded.

Meredith held the chain over the pieces of paper and the ring between her fingers. The perfume bottle sat next to the candle.

"Are you the spirit who haunts this house?"

Time appeared to slow as they stared unblinking at the crystal hovering over the piece of paper with "Yes" written on it. Ever so slowly, it began to move in a clockwise direction.

Emma's throat dried up. "What does that mean?" she managed to croak.

"Clockwise is an affirmative response. In the Northern hemisphere anyway."

Emma went silent once more.

Meredith drew a deep breath and continued. "Did you used to live in this house?"

The pendulum swung again in the same direction. Emma felt her body crawl with a layer of perspiration. In just a few short days, her entire world had turned upside down and now she was communicating with a ghost, through a friend who was a medium. No one would have believed her except Meredith.

"Did you die in this house?"

Once again, the pendulum swung in a clockwise direction. Meredith met Emma's gaze for a moment.

"The next few bits might not be so nice," Meredith warned. "But you won't come to any harm, I promise."

Emma tried to feel reassured.

"Did you die as a result of illness?"

This time the pendulum remained still over the "Yes" paper, so Meredith held it over "No". It jerked a little then swung in a clockwise direction.

"So," – Emma hesitated a little – "she didn't die of an illness?"

"It would appear not."

Meredith concentrated on the pendulum again.

"Did you die at someone else's hand?"

Emma's heart skipped a beat. Again the answer was no.

"Did you take your own life?"

This time the answer was yes. A chilly breeze filled the room. The ring, which Emma had placed on the table, began to twitch. The perfume bottle wobbled slightly, then became still again. The candle flickered but remained lit. Emma's eyes were glued to the scene before her. She could hear her heartbeat in her head like a bass drum. Meredith met her eyes again.

"Are you OK for me to continue?"

Emma thought for a moment and nodded again.

"I have to know what happened, so I can help her, right?"

Meredith smiled at her, tilting her head sympathetically. She paused before continuing. "The ring on the table. Did it belong to you?"

Yes.

"Was it a wedding ring?"

No.

Another cold draught blew through the room. The candle went out and both girls shivered.

"I feel angry suddenly," Meredith said. "Well, it's kind of a mixture between anger and sadness. She's trying to make me feel her own feelings. She's haunting by emotion. Heartbreak, that's it. Her heart was broken. I suspect that's why she chose you, because of your break-up. She knew you'd understand."

"Did your husband love someone else?"

No.

"Did you love someone else?"

Yes.

"Emma, you said the ring was likely to have been unworn. It was not a wedding ring, but it was given out of love." Meredith looked up at the ceiling. "Am I correct?"

Yes.

"Was the man you loved already married to someone else?"

No.

"Oh, of course!" Realisation dawned on Meredith's face. "Were you in love with a woman?"

Yes.

Meredith breathed deeply. "I think we're getting somewhere." She shifted position so she sat cross-legged on the floor by the table. Emma did the same, aware that her legs were becoming uncomfortable.

"You were betrothed to a man against your will?"

Yes.

"Did your family find out about your lover?"

Yes.

"They didn't like it, did they?"

No.

"Oh!" Meredith suddenly burst into tears and clutched at her breast.

"Are you okay?"

Tears rolled down Meredith's cheeks. "She's so sad!" she sobbed. "They must have been very much in love but couldn't be together. Em, I'm so sorry, I have to stop. This is exhausting."

"Sure, no worries."

"We need to burn the papers. Best to light your fire and throw them on."

"Can I ask one final question?" Emma stared at the ceiling this time, wondering if she could be heard too. "Is your name Grace?"

Yes.

Chapter Sixteen

Emma cleaned away the remnants of the séance while Meredith sipped herbal tea and stared into the dying embers of the paper notes.

"I've never felt that before. Never had ..." Meredith took another sip, as if willing herself to speak. "I've never experienced a spirit's emotions before. I thought I was going to be washed away by some invisible tide of tears. It was awful. So very, very sad." She paused for a moment. "I don't think I've ever felt that level of sadness myself. What about you? Oh, shit."

Emma was sat on the sofa next to her, deep in her own thoughts and reminiscing about the tragedy she had herself experienced only months before. She struggled with tears as she turned round.

"Darling, I didn't think. I'm so sorry."

Emma sank into her friend's shoulder and sobbed her heart out.

Months of frustration and the stress of moving house, the agony of starting her life all over again – it all came to the surface. She wasn't prepared to be alone, to be lonely. She thought she was breaking apart inside.

Meredith was silent, thank God. She wasn't stupid enough to have to ask the cause of her pain. She knew very well. After some time, she began to calm down. Details of the last few weeks, preparing for the move, had come flooding back to her, things she had pushed to the back of her mind until this moment, when she could finally allow herself to reflect upon her predicament. She remembered the wedding gifts she had thrown away, the honeymoon photographs, the trinkets Paul had bought for her when they had first fallen in love. All gone, lost in a different world.

She was glad to have moved house though. The marital home held too many memories. Shadows had lurked in every corner, making her feel confined. She would never have been able to rebuild her life there. She already felt at home in this little cottage, despite it being already occupied.

Most of all, she regretted the pain her parents had had to endure too. For them, marriage break-up was one of those things that happened to other people. Her mother in particular was hurt, and she barely told a soul among her circle of friends.

Emma had a sudden longing for a sibling, someone who shared her upbringing, someone who could help her. She was grateful to have a friend like Meredith, yes, but Meredith had two brothers and a sister. She didn't know what being an only child was like.

Meredith planted a kiss on her forehead.

"Honey, I really should go now. I said I'd visit my mother. I think Grace will be okay for tonight. I suspect she's probably shedding her own tears in the astral plane somewhere. If you need me, call and I can escape. Don't sit here and sob your heart out alone."

Emma coughed. "Thank you so much. For everything."

"Hey, thank *you*. This is a learning experience for me too. We have more to learn about dear Grace, but now we know who she is, perhaps you can do a little research and we can find out why she's still here in this world. I'll have a think about the next steps on a spiritual level. You, my lovely, need to get some rest."

***

Emma relaxed into the indulgent, fizzing soap suds with an audible moan of pleasure.

"Oh, this feels so wonderful, Lily."

The cat blinked from her perch on the wicker linen basket and nonchalantly licked a paw.

"Well, I guess baths aren't really your thing, are they?"

Emma took another sip of wine and giggled.

"I think I deserve this, I really do."

She missed her life as a married woman. Not Paul. She didn't miss him at all, but she hated coming home to an empty house after a stressful day at work, with no one's arms to fall into. Companionship. That was what she missed most of all.

Her mind wandered back to Lewis. Perhaps her hot neighbour would fill the gap in her life? The night they had spent together had been hasty, she knew, but she didn't regret it one little bit. In fact, it had made her feel so wonderful again, after the heartbreak of Paul. She did regret the fact that he lived next door though. How was she going to face him again after that?

***

The doorbell rang just as dusk was settling on the village. Even before she got to the door, Emma knew it was Lewis.

She hesitated a little before letting him in, studying his face for clues as to whether he was disappointed in her.

"I'm really sorry." It was all she could say.

They sat down on the sofa and she took his hand and stroked it.

"I'm so not ready for a relationship right now," she said eventually.

"Me neither." Lewis looked relieved.

"Something has happened which has made me question some things and also brought back a lot of painful memories and emotions."

She took a deep breath. Lewis sat in silence, patiently waiting for her to continue. After a long pause, she decided just to tell him everything.

She started with the ring, the perfume and the seduction. She left out most of the details, except that it had felt like a human, not some kind of ethereal being from another dimension, and definitely not dead.

She told him about what had happened with Meredith and her breakdown afterwards. She mentioned how Grace's story had given her a chance to focus on someone else and not get too bogged down in herself.

Lewis listened carefully, staring at her. She couldn't tell if he believed her or not, but she considered that to be his problem, not hers.

"Well, I think you're right about not wanting a relationship," he said eventually. "There's way too much other stuff going on here."

He took a sip of coffee and breathed a deep sigh.

"Friends?"

Emma beamed with delight.

"Yes, I'd like that, of course!"

"In which case, it's high time I was heading home. You go back to work in a few days, yes? So, let's try and get to the bottom of this mystery before then. That is, if you'd like me to help?"

"That would be great, thanks."

Emma smiled in genuine gratitude. It had been easier than she had expected, but something didn't feel quite right. Her head knew she'd made the right decision, but what of her heart? It seemed to be remaining tight-lipped on the matter for now. She would just have to work it out herself.

***

Lewis seems such a nice guy, she thought. But the timing is all wrong. I'm not ready for this.

She pictured his face – the rugged good looks of someone old enough to have gained some maturity, but young enough to still have plenty of vitality. Then there was that little sparkle in his eye, which she was becoming increasingly fond of and found strangely reassuring.

One thing was nagging at her though. She cast her mind back to the telephone argument she had overheard. Who was the 'Annabelle' he was shouting at? An ex-girlfriend, perhaps? If so, were things really over between them?

She was also touched that he was taking time out to help her with the mystery of Grace. A thought crossed her mind: did it mean he had an ulterior motive? She pushed the idea away. That was how you became bitter and twisted, having thoughts like that. She'd seen it happen with some of her friends' mothers. Couple gets divorced; man finds another partner with relative ease; woman spends the rest of her life turning into a grumpy old woman and develops a biting cynicism to the point where she becomes unlovable.

In a moment of clarity, Emma realised that was actually her deepest fear. She wanted to be loved. She did not want to transform into one of those contemptuous and scornful women she knew.

There wasn't time for all this reflection just now, though. The sun was setting and she was painfully aware that Grace's mystery remained unresolved.

Chapter Seventeen

Inside the old village library there was a hint of mustiness in the air. A wry smile came to Emma's lips as she recalled her first impressions of Anthony's antique shop. How appropriate that his wife's place of work should invoke similar sensations.

"Hey, Claire."

"Oh, Emma, how lovely to see you!" Claire looked genuinely delighted as she carried a pile of hardback books to a nearby trolley. "Were you looking for something to help you in your project, perhaps?"

"Well, yes, I have some more information about the girl. About Grace."

Claire placed the pile of books on the trolley and locked the barrier behind her.

"You're lucky, it's not that busy today. Tell me what you've found."

"Well, my source isn't that reliable, but I'd like to check out what I've learned nonetheless." Emma bit her lip. "You may remember I said my house is haunted?"

"I do, my dear, but I did wonder whether it was the stress of moving that brought it on. Are you saying there's more to it than that?"

"Well, a friend of mine is a medium and we held a séance thing to contact her. It's definitely that Grace you mentioned. It turns out she was due to be married but couldn't go through with it because she was in love with a woman. Her family didn't approve and, well, she committed suicide."

"I see." Claire looked at her for a moment. Emma wondered if she'd said too much.

"Well, it would explain the scandal my grandmother went on about, and why I struggled to find out much during my own investigations. But then, I wasn't researching her specifically. Nevertheless, it is a clue, as you say, regardless of its dubious source, and therefore, it needs to be verified. Come with me."

She led them towards the back of the library and into a smaller room, with desks and lamps provided for research purposes.

"I'd really like to help but I'm on my own today. Normally there are two of us, you see. Let me show you the local history section, and in the meantime I have a registrar friend who may be able to offer some guidance so I shall call them and come back to you."

After a couple of hours, Emma was nearing the limit of her patience when she found a small footnote in one volume quite by accident. She would have missed it had the photograph of the cottage not grabbed her attention like a firm but invisible grip on her shoulder.

It read: *The last blacksmith to inhabit Horseshoe Cottage, Joe Richardson, left around 1786. It was rumoured that he was unable to continue the business after the tragic death of his daughter, Grace, and he lived out his days in solitude.*

"Cracking impression of a Venus Flytrap," said a voice behind her. "I thought I might find you here."

Emma jumped and quickly closed her gaping mouth.

Lewis stood looking down at her and smiled. God, those eyes would be the death of her.

"Look at this." She turned the book for him to read as he sat down at the desk.

"Oh, cool. This is your place."

"Yes. Read what it says."

Lewis scanned the piece. "Oh. I see."

Luckily, the front desk was quiet.

"Oh! How sad," Claire said. "Sounds like she did come to an untimely end after all. Poor girl." She thought for a moment, then added, "My own family members are buried in the churchyard not far from your house. The church has been there several hundred years, so it contains some very old headstones. Although, of course, if she did indeed commit suicide, she's unlikely to be there."

Emma looked puzzled.

"You see, in those days suicide victims weren't buried in consecrated ground. She would have been laid to rest elsewhere. Some churchyards left a corner for such poor souls, but not all of them. It is possible you may never find her, to be honest."

Emma was in a daze. She hadn't considered the possibility that she may never find Grace's remains. Would the ghost haunt her for ever?

"Sometimes, suicide victims were buried at a crossroads outside the village," Claire went on. "The idea was that if or when their spirit rose, they would be confused and be unsure of the correct way home. The churchyard was the hub of the village."

Emma nodded slowly, trying to take it all in.

"I'm sorry, Emma. You must be prepared for that." Claire's nose squirmed slightly before she continued, "And, of course, there are all these ridiculous housing developments which seem to be shooting up all over the place. They'll be dredging up all sorts of things, no doubt. Young married people can't afford to come and live here. The whole place will be an early graveyard before long."

A customer came to the desk and the conversation ceased. Emma retreated with Lewis in tow. Claire had been hugely helpful and had given her a useful perspective on the situation.

Chapter Eighteen

Once back at the cottage, Emma's spine prickled. Despite the enjoying her tryst with Grace, she didn't want to be haunted by her soul for ever. She wanted to put her to rest, somehow.

Emma turned to Lewis and found he was just about to open his mouth too.

"You first," he said.

Well, I'm at a loss where to go next, to be honest. Like Claire said, what if I never find Grace? What then? If Claire is correct and she was buried alone, I thought the best way would be to find her and put her back into the churchyard. How can I do that if we don't find any remains?"

"I don't know, Em. You're the one with the link to her. Why don't you ask?"

Emma thought for a moment. She had the distinct impression that he wasn't telling her everything, but chose to keep the feeling to herself.

"Sure, no problem. I'll try the church. Just in case."

She saw him out of the door and made her own way towards the village church.

As expected, the records brought up no one by the name of Grace Richardson. The vicar had helpfully told her that he had a good record of everyone who lay there and that her name was not among them, and would not have been if indeed she had taken her own life. Her father, however, was laid to rest there, and his headstone remained in good condition, perhaps because it was sheltered from the weather by a huge oak tree. Reverend Dickinson could offer them no information about where else in the village a person might be buried.

"I need to start thinking about work again in a couple of days," she thought, after the door had closed. "It would be really nice if everything was done and dusted by then."

That night, she reminisced over the erotic encounter with Grace and admitted to herself she would in fact be disappointed if it didn't happen again. With her heart pounding and her fingers trembling as she undressed, Emma got into bed naked and waited.

She must have dozed eventually, despite her nervous excitement, for she woke with a start some time later.

She recognised a chill in the air and the now-familiar floral fragrance. It was little surprise when her eyelids opened that the first thing she saw was Grace's spirit, still shimmering, sitting on the edge of the bed and smiling at her.

Emma sat up slowly, fearing that if she moved too quickly, the beautiful apparition would disappear.

"H-h-hello," she whispered.

Grace leaned forward and stroked her cheek. Emma reached out to hold her hand. She longed to know more about Grace's story, but didn't want to scare her away.

"I have thought about you," Emma said. "I went to learn about you and found out about your father."

Grace's head fell and she started to cry. Emma was overwhelmed by an intense wave of melancholy and she recalled Meredith's emotional state during the séance.

"You communicate with emotion?" Emma said.

All of a sudden, Grace's face sparkled with animation. She nodded and a huge grin crossed her face. Emma felt her own heart lift with joy. Still holding Grace's hand, she brought it to her lips to kiss.

"I really want to help you but I need more clues. What is it you're searching for?"

Grace put a finger to Emma's lips to hush her, then replaced it with her own lips. Emma inhaled deeply, as if to drink in the all-consuming passion she felt the spirit was transmitting through her tongue as it delved deeper inside her mouth.

Once again, Emma lay back and allowed herself to be seduced, caressed, stroked and pleasured to orgasm, her soul surrendering to the blissful release. When the tide of emotion subsided, she started to kiss Grace again but the ghost turned away, much to Emma's surprise. Instead, Grace lay down next to her and held her, gently stroking her head until she fell fast asleep.

***

It was still dark when Emma woke and she was groggy. She was being shaken, quite roughly, by the arm.

"Get up, Emma!"

Grace, perfectly formed like any ordinary human being and speaking in full voice, was standing next to her bed. "Hurry!" she said. "We haven't got long!"

Emma mumbled something and then she was dressed and standing on her own front doorstep. The cold shook her fully awake soon enough.

"What on earth am I doing here?"

"It's alright," Grace replied. "You're asleep and dreaming. It's the only way I can show you. Hurry up."

Grace skipped ahead and Emma followed. It occurred to Emma that something felt different about the village. She was relieved for the moonlight, at least, although it was slipping towards the horizon. They arrived at a small building at the back of the cottage where there was a glow from inside and the sound of men's voices could be heard. Emma realised she couldn't remember putting her feet on the ground.

Grace took Emma by the hand and they peeked around the door frame to look inside. Emma could not believe the scene in front of her. Grace – beautiful, sensual, captivating Grace – was hanging from a noose in the centre of the room. A fire raged in one corner and Emma realised this must have been the forge. A man in a loose white shirt and a leather apron was turned away from the body and staring into the fire. An older man and another, much younger, man were in the process of cutting the rope.

Emma threw her hand to her mouth to cover her gasp.

"That's how I did it," came a whisper from beside her. "Come on, no time to lose!"

Wide-eyed and speechless with fright, Emma allowed Grace to grab her hand again, and they ran up the road to the heart of the village, to the old inn. Emma turned to look back but the glow from the building had gone.

"Time is different here," Grace explained.

Grace kept running, and Emma kept up behind her, not wishing to get left behind or miss anything. They stopped outside what appeared to be the inn. A colourful sign hung above the door. There was some commotion inside. A young woman was sitting at a table, sobbing and wearing what appeared to be a nightgown. A group of people were on the other side of the room, apparently chatting amongst themselves and not wishing to be heard by the sorrowful girl.

A man strode over to her. "You can't be getting all upset like this, Suzanne. Grace was your friend, of course, but folks will think this is too much, under the circumstances."

Emma looked at Grace, who had gone silent.

"Is that her?"

Grace nodded, then took her hand and off they went again, leaving the village a travelling until there were no more buildings, just trees and fields.

"Nearly there!" Grace said. She stopped at a crossroads. "Here we are."

She walked over to a hedgerow and pulled back a few branches. The full moon appeared from behind a cloud and shone directly onto the spot. There, among the gorse and blackberry bushes, was an iron cross.

"This is where I am. You have to find me. I have to be with my Pa. I have to tell him how sorry I am."

The moon shone brighter still, it seemed, and Emma could make out the tears welling up in Grace's eyes. She moved towards her for an embrace, but Grace pulled away again.

"It's time to go now. Close your eyes and I'll take you home."

Chapter Nineteen

Dawn revealed an overcast sky. There was rain in the air, for sure. Emma sent a text to Lewis and pulled the covers close around her shoulders, cursing the British summer weather.

> *What time are you coming over today? Could use your help. Have had … inspiration.*

She yawned and pressed Send, then replaced the handset on the bedside table and contemplated going back to sleep, mainly to try and memorise the scenes from her dream. But really there was no need; she would forget nothing she had seen any time soon. The image of the small iron cross, likely forged by Grace's poor father in the midst of unimaginable grief, stuck in her mind the most.

She was still in something of a daze when Lewis turned up on her doorstep an hour later.

"What's this all about then?"

"We're taking a walk to the building site on the edge of town," she said. "I need to check something."

Lewis was sensible enough to keep his mouth shut and followed her out the door. He offered to carry her umbrella, but was less keen when it came to the shovel.

"Are you really sure about that? People talk around here, you know."

"Yeah, well they don't know me yet, so it's not like I have a reputation to destroy. This way, they'll be wary to start with and all I can do is improve."

Lewis said nothing, but he trailed behind her as they marched up towards the development site on the edge of the village. As usual the sound of machinery and heavy plant vehicles filled the air.

Emma stopped at the crossroads and looked about her, turning exactly ninety degrees and looking left and right at each turn. Lewis stood back and watched.

I don't care if he thinks I'm crazy, she thought. Hell, maybe I am. Today, I don't care.

"I think it's this corner," she declared over the noise of the tractor in a nearby field. Out of her bag she pulled two pairs of gardening gloves. "Here you go."

Lewis took them reluctantly. "I didn't realise this would involve manual labour, Emma. I normally get paid for stuff like this."

"It'll be quicker if we both do it, and we'll get less wet."

He couldn't fault her logic, so he knelt in the grassy verge next to her and started pulling away the brambles. After half an hour's work, they had made little progress.

"You know I'm a handyman, right? I could have brought my power tools to save us both this frankly rather strenuous work."

"Too risky. Might damage the evidence." Emma paused and knelt up again, putting a hand to her aching back.

"Should I ask how you know about this?"

"Probably not."

Another half an hour passed and still they unearthed nothing. The noises from the building site seemed to have ceased. Lewis got to his knees and groaned.

"I have an idea, but I'm going to need your help this time."

Emma looked up at him as he held out a hand. Gratefully, she took it. They were both more than a little muddy, and the damp weather was making them both tired and miserable.

Lewis walked ahead this time, and they came to a small Portakabin on the building site.

"Hi guys." Lewis poked his head around the door, which was propped open with a breeze block. "Wonder if you could help us? My friend and I are doing a bit of detective work but the weather's come down and we're both freezing. You couldn't give us a cup of hot tea, could you?"

Emma had to admire the balls of the man. Such confidence! She shrank behind the door to remain unseen, waiting for the answer. She heard someone rise to their feet.

"Aye, lad, no problems. The boss is out at the minute, otherwise he'd be sending you away. This isn't for visiting by the public, you know, but it is awful out there. Sit yerselves down. I'll see if we've got a couple of mugs."

The steaming tea arrived just a few moments later.

"What kind of work did you say you were doing?"

Emma's brain suddenly engaged. "Hi," she said, poking her head around the door.

A group of three blokes sat on cheap-looking desks littered with paperwork. The walls of the cabin were covered with what appeared to be project plans and some technical drawings detailing the development plans.

"I'm actually doing a bit of family history research and, well, I'm trying to find a, erm, well, I'm looking for …"

"A body. We're looking for a body." The words tumbled out of Lewis's mouth almost without his thinking, it seemed.

The workmen's mouths fell open and they glanced at each other nervously.

A fourth man came through from a side door and held out his hand.

"Rob Thornton, site manager. A body, you say? I may well be able to help you if you'd like to come into my office?"

The workmen quickly shuffled papers and sat up straight at their desks. Clearly this was the boss who they hadn't been expecting.

"Ah, Lewis, isn't it? I remember you from the pub."

The two men shook hands.

"Family history, did you say?" Rob motioned them to sit in the two chairs in front of his desk. "Seems to be all the rage these days."

"You said you might be able to help?" Emma was eager to find out as much she could while they were there.

"Do you have a connection with the deceased?" Rob looked concerned. It was understandable, perhaps. After all, they could have been anyone. Emma looked at the floor briefly, trying to compose herself and not give anything away.

"If it is who I think it is, then yes, I believe I do."

Rob looked out of the Portakabin window. He seemed distant.

"Rob? You okay?" Lewis seemed just as keen as Emma to get him to divulge information.

After another pause and a heavy sigh, Rob put his mug of tea down on the desk and leaned forward. "I haven't told this to any of the lads. They would never believe me anyway. It all started the day the diggers arrived. We had marked out the verge, right by the crossroads as the main focus of the first phase. We can't really start building the houses until there's a road structure of sorts, you see." Another pause. "So the digger started up and it was all going well until a few hours later. I was in here, I remember, making a tea, when I heard all this commotion outside. So, I grabbed my hard hat and went to see what was going on."

His voice reduced to a whisper, as if he didn't want to give the thought credibility by putting it into words. "And ... there it was."

Emma could see the man trembling as he picked up his mug again, only to peer inside at the emptiness. He slammed it down on the table. Whatever had happened to this man had left him shocked and unstable.

"Would you mind if I got a fresh cup of tea? It's been a long day."

Lewis and Emma exchanged glances after Rob left for the makeshift kitchen. Whatever was on his mind, Emma really wanted him to blurt it all out so she could get out of there as quickly as possible. The whole place felt very uncomfortable all of a sudden.

Rob returned, sat down, took a large gulp from the fresh mug and smiled at her. She saw vulnerability in him.

"Please, Rob, just tell us what you know." She tried to sound pleading, hoping it would help.

His face crumpled. He squeezed his eyes shut, as if hoping that when he opened them, Emma and Lewis would no longer be there. When he looked back at Emma, he swallowed hard and bit his lip. "It haunts me."

His whisper echoed in Emma's mind. Her head snapped around to face Lewis and they stared at each other in disbelief. A dozen questions swam in her mind, but from what she had seen and heard so far, getting more from Rob would not be easy. "Me too," she whispered. "If it's the same ghost."

Her eyes lifted to Rob's, uncertain of his reaction. How much should she tell him?

"Really?"

The distance between them had shrunk such that Emma could make out the aroma of stale sweat and earth on him. She nodded in response, then watched as a weak smile crossed his face.

"Then I'm not going mad? Oh, thank God for that. You have no idea what this means to me."

Rob checked his mobile phone then turned back to face Emma.

"So she's a relative of yours, then?" he asked.

"Oh, no. It turns out she used to live in the cottage where I moved to just a couple weeks ago."

"It's a she, then?" Rob raised his eyebrows.

"Well, yes. Can't you tell?"

Perhaps it wasn't the same ghost after all. Maybe the village was full of unsettled spirits.

"It's not obvious, no."

He hung back then, and Emma sensed she needed an explanation for the strangeness she now felt. "What do you see when the ghost appears, Rob?"

"It's always the same, like some horror movie, to be honest. But, essentially, it's exactly as I found her. A skeleton, with the neck broken. One of the arms is reaching out towards me. It's as if it wants to strangle me." He paused again, and took another gulp of tea. "There's a laugh too, it laughs at me. It sounds like a lunatic. Then I wake up."

He began to tremble again, so Emma placed a hand on his arm. After a couple more deep breaths, he composed himself. "So what do you see?" he asked.

Emma smiled and turned to Lewis, who nodded in encouragement. She would have to be careful here. Revealing too much could appear anything but genuine.

She recalled Grace's sad, forlorn face the first time she saw her, then the arousal, lust and passion of subsequent occasions. "She's really quite beautiful to me. I suppose I see her as though she's not really dead." She thought for a moment. "Did you say you found her?"

"The diggers uncovered what was left of a coffin and some human remains. The wood was mostly rotted away, so the bones were visible. It was quite a shallow grave, see. I haven't slept much since then."

Emma jumped out of the chair and leapt to hug a stunned Rob. "Oh, but this is wonderful! Don't you see? What happened to the coffin? Where is she?"

"How the hell should I know? The coroner's office came to collect the remains and they spent a whole day on site, looking for 'evidence', or so they said. All I know is that my project is now way behind schedule. Look, if you're that bothered, I can give you the name of the guy at the council who I spoke to. He might know."

"Rob, thank you so much! You've made my day. No, in fact, my entire week."

As she ran out of the room, closely followed by Lewis, she turned and beamed an enormous smile back at Rob. "You know, this might even resolve your crazy dreams too."

***

Emma stood in front of the full-length mirror with a frustrated expression on her face. She had flung her third and final pair of jeans onto the floor. It was ridiculous. How many people got upset when they *lost* weight? She should be jumping for joy, but the simple fact was that none of her jeans now fitted her. She hated wearing skirts and therefore owned none, which left only her work trousers. Luckily, she found a pair that still fit her. She was sliding them over her hips when the doorbell rang. Lewis was early.

The daylight apparition staring back at her when she opened the door wore a weak smile.

"Can we talk?" Lewis's voice was almost a whisper.

Chapter Twenty

February 1785

"How can I ever go on, Reverend?"

"Now, Joe, you're a good man. You mustn't talk like this."

Reverend Harrison placed a calming hand on the man's shoulder but it did little to lighten his heavy heart. His only daughter had gone, by her own hand, and it was his fault. If only he had had the courage to sit down with her and talk properly, instead of choosing to ignore her predicament.

His wife's face came to his mind. Poor, dear Anna. How would she have dealt with this? Since Anna's death, Grace had grown into her image and he had found it so hard to have a relationship with his daughter, so alike were they. Now, because of his stubbornness, he had lost them both. Curses on him!

"Whatever shall I do, Reverend?"

"The Lord works in mysterious ways, Joe. You know that. You're a good, pious man. He knows you have the strength for this. Pray with me."

"I don't know if I can. I have lost the will for such things."

"Well, then kneel here with me now, and I'll do the praying for us both."

Joe looked at the bowed head of the local vicar and sighed. He slipped to his knees and bowed his head, but his heart wasn't in it. Reverend Harrison had been so helpful, sitting with him every night by the fire, listening to his troubled soul or just sitting in silence. It brought him some comfort. For a man so used to solitude, he had recently found he didn't want to be alone.

***

Some days later, Joe was shuffling back from the forge to make himself lunch. Recent events had aged him and he looked much older than his fifty-two years. Hunched over the dining table with his meagre bread and soup, he almost didn't see the Reverend come into the house, much less the petite creature who followed him.

Her long raven-coloured hair framed a beautiful but grief-stricken face.

"Joe, I've brought someone to see you."

"I have no interest in talking to her!"

There was an uncomfortable silence, which Reverend Harrison broke with a cough. "Now then, Joe. That's not a Christian way to treat another human being. Remember, Suzanne is also grieving." He turned to the girl and encouraged her to speak. "She has something she would like to say, I think, don't you, girl?"

"Mr. Richardson, sir?" She shuffled over towards the wooden table where Joe sat. He sat up and folded his arms, his disdain for her obvious in his expression. "I have come to tell you that Tom and I are to be married and we shall be leaving Fosbury for Oxfordshire. Under the circumstances, I didn't think you would want me staying in the village, so I think it's for the best."

Joe remained silent.

"She speaks sense, Joe. You must see that," the Reverend said gently. "It will be a quiet ceremony, one which I shall conduct myself, and they will be gone by the end of the month. Then we can try and put this whole sorry business behind us."

Joe nodded slowly. Reverend Harrison ushered the girl out the door, her part having been fulfilled, and took a seat next to Joe at the table. Neither man said anything for a few moments.

"Is there more soup, Joe?"

Another nod.

"I'll help myself then, shall I?"

"Aye."

Lunch continued in silence, and Joe stood to collect the empty bowls when they'd finished. Reverend Harrison was about to take his leave when Joe called him back.

"Reverend, will you call again tomorrow evening? Perhaps you would bring Tom and Suzanne with you. I may have something for them."

The vicar raised an eyebrow. "Of course, Joe. Yes, I will. Take care."

***

The following evening, Tom, Suzanne and the Reverend sat in parlour of the small cottage. Joe stood on the hearth, trying to find the right words. Anna would have had the eloquence to deliver this much better than he. "I don't want to keep you folks long, so I'll not tarry." He coughed. He had started now, so he had to get it over with. "I want to thank you, Suzanne, for coming to see me yesterday. That was a brave thing. I agree that it would be for the best if you leave the village."

He turned to Tom, until lately his young apprentice. "Tom, I have a friend near where you are moving to, a farrier by the name of Archie Wilson. He'll see you right.

"Suzanne, Grace loved you very much, I see that now. The best thing I can do for her is make sure that you are provided for. I have a little money put aside. It was meant as a wedding gift for Grace, of course. She would want you to be happy, and I mean to see that you start your married life with some means. It's not much, but it's what she would have wanted."

He took a deep breath and swallowed his ale in one gulp, as if it gave him fortitude. "That's all I had to say."

A somewhat stunned Reverend Harrison got to his feet. He joined his friend by the hearth and shook his hand. "Grace would be so proud of you, Joe," he said. "She is smiling down on you now, I know it."

Joe nodded and turned away. They must not see how hard that had been for him to say those words; they must not see the tears collecting in the corners of his eyes.

He had to admit to himself, though, that it felt much better to be kind in the face of tragedy. He had spent much too long ruminating of late, thinking of the past. It was his own stupid fault he was alone now. Best not to make things worse.

Chapter Twenty-One

"Is this about that telephone argument a few days ago?"

Emma couldn't believe the bravado in her own voice and gasped, putting her hand over her mouth.

Lewis glanced back at her, then at the floor. There was something about his demeanour which made all this feel wrong. Something had happened.

She let him in and they moved towards the sofa in silence. Lewis fell almost deadweight into the fabric, as if the life from him had vanished.

"You heard it then?" Lewis cleared his throat. "I guess I owe you an explanation."

"Lewis, it's fine. We're just friends now, remember?"

"No, it's not fine. I need to tell you what's been going on. Will you let me explain?"

Emma nodded. His face looked tortured. Gone was the charisma she had adored from the start, replaced by a vulnerability that in other men would have been a deal-breaker. In Lewis though, it melted a place in her heart she had thought long dead. Her nurturing instinct kicked in and she laid a hand on his thigh. He looked up at her and into her eyes, searching for reassurance.

"Go on, I'm listening."

"I wanted you from the first time I laid eyes on you. Normally, I get what I want, but then it turns out to be nothing like I imagined. I knew you would be different.

"I had hoped to woo you properly, but that night at the pub, you looked so beautifully helpless, I couldn't hold myself back. I knew you would run away emotionally afterwards, and you did exactly that. I'm sorry for scaring you like that."

Emma held her breath for the next statement but nothing came from Lewis. He bit his lip and stared at the floor.

"Lewis, that's lovely, but I don't see what your feelings for me have to do with that argument. Who's Annabelle?"

"Emma, I'm not who you think I am. I need to come clean."

***

Emma stood outside the corporate-grey building and peered in through the door, mulling over whether she should walk in and greet her colleagues or run away.

She had taken two weeks off to move house, but so much had happened that it felt like a lifetime. Most of it she couldn't possibly explain to any of the rabble in here anyway; they would never understand.

She took a deep breath and pulled open the door.

"Hey, Em! Great to see you, lovely!" Oh, no. Maxine had spotted her already and came running over to hug her. "Oh, I'm so glad you're back. Steve's been struggling while you've been away and tried to throw a load of your work onto me but, oh, you know how it is, I barely have the time to do my own thing. Oh, and then the second week, Josh was ill with chicken pox, would you believe, so I had to stay home and look after him."

Emma recalled Maxine's endless tales of woe about her only son. Maxine mollycoddled the poor child so much, Emma dreaded to think what kind of man he would grow up to become.

"Then, Gerard's wife went into labour the other day, so we won't see him for another week or so. It's a girl, by the way, seven pound something. Mum and baby all okay. So you've missed all sorts really. How was your house move?"

Emma stared back at Maxine, wondering whether she had always had verbal diarrhoea or if she was just really excited to see her. She had no idea how to respond to the onslaught of information, so she chose to keep it simple. "It was good, thanks."

Maxine took the cue and moved out of the way while Emma scuttled over to her desk.

"Anyway, I'll let you get settled back in. There's a team meeting at eleven, so you'll have a chance to catch up then."

Emma thought it would take more than a team meeting to catch up on everything, but she smiled back nonetheless.

***

The next few days proved busy enough, giving Emma plenty to distract her from both Grace's predicament and her own feelings of emptiness whenever she thought about Lewis.

His revelations had given her much cause for reflection. Lewis's wealthy but estranged father had been found dead in his office. Turned out their last argument had exacerbated his existing heart condition. The final straw had been a falling out with his PA, the infamous Annabelle, and she had taken to throwing things at him, setting off the final, massive heart attack.

Lewis's solicitor had called to let him know that his father's will had been redrafted to include him after all, which made him the sole beneficiary. Annabelle was nowhere to be found, but it was thought that she had discovered the details of the will, hence the argument.

It was an awful lot to take in, and her head told her it would be wise to steer clear until the dust had settled.

As far as her other concern, the council had promised a response to the application for reburial within seven days, and Emma was not a patient person. When she woke on Saturday morning to the squeaky letterbox and a loud splat on the doormat, she was relieved they'd stuck to their word. She rushed downstairs and tore it open. The word "Granted" was stamped across the photocopied application form.

She texted Meredith immediately.

"It's arrived. We're on."

"I'll be round in an hour."

A few days later

The coffin seemed to take an age to lower into the ground. Emma took a moment to glance around at the attendees. Anthony and Claire had both dressed head to toe in black. Even Claire's delicate handkerchief, which she used to gently dab her cheeks, was black.

Rob Thornton looked relieved more than anything. Emma cast her mind back to their exchange at his site office. The man staring at the grave looked weather-beaten, but she had a feeling he would sleep better at night from now on. Their eyes met. His smile was weak but genuine and she smiled back.

He stood next to the council representative, who wore an expression of utter boredom. Clearly this was a non-event for him, a formality to make sure the job was done.

As seemed appropriate for such an occasion, the sky was a dull grey. Meredith stood next to Emma, holding her hand and trying not to cry too much. She wore her spiritual robes, in a mixture of blue and purple. It was to cover both tranquillity and transformation, she said, which would assist Grace's spirit in passing on to be reconciled with her father.

Lewis looked every part the dashing suitor in a sharp black suit and tie, and her stomach lurched as he glanced back at her and smiled. It would be his father's funeral too the following day. What a week for him. She mused over what would happen between them next.

But today wasn't about her relationship with Lewis; today was all about Grace. Poor dead, restless Grace, whose spirit had been unsettled for over two hundred years, waiting for someone who felt the depth of emotion that she felt, to solve her story and finally lay her to rest.

The vicar finished up and the three of them murmured some acknowledgement. In her heart, Emma felt more at ease than she had in several weeks. "I vote we go to the pub and raise a glass to dear Grace," she said as they walked out of the churchyard.

"Sounds good to me." Lewis smiled, clearly more comfortable with the idea of a log fire than the dank sky, which was growing darker by the minute.

"I need to be off, darling, I'm sorry." Meredith kissed her on the cheek and winked. "I'm sure I can trust you two to make sure she has a good wake though!"

Weekday evenings in the pub weren't quite so busy as weekends but there was still a lively crowd, and the hubbub meant they could chat easily about nothing too important. Emma felt the conversation come to her much more easily every time she spoke with Lewis.

"I think you will sleep better tonight than you have done in some time," Lewis announced.

"I think you're right, I will. It's been a rollercoaster, that's for sure."

Lewis laid an arm on hers and smiled. "I have a favour to ask, and I have a question. I don't know which to start with."

Emma thought for a moment and smirked. "How about you start with the question? Depending on what it is, then I can decide whether I feel like doing any favours for you."

He laughed. "Okay, the question is: have you thought about what I said the other day, about my feelings for you? I want us to be together, Emma, and I think it will be great. I can't promise you it'll be perfect, but I won't leave you, I promise."

Time stood still. She had been well aware of this man's impact on her life so far, and how attracted she was to him. Living next door, she had been reticent to acknowledge that the arrangement couldn't be more perfect, in case it all went wrong and she was left with an acrimonious neighbour.

She allowed herself to agree that they were in fact very well suited. He had been frank with her about his past at last, which had opened her heart enough for her to trust him.

She gazed into his eyes, took his hand and squeezed.

"I think we could be great too."

***

Emma didn't know what time it was, or even if she was properly awake rather than dreaming again, but there was a familiar coldness in her bedroom. Her heart sank. Grace had been reburied so what was the reason for this?

As Grace materialised in front of her eyes, though, she felt her emotions taken over once again. Instead of sadness, however, this time there was joy and peace, and another figure stood next to her. Emma had to squint a little to see properly. It was another girl with very long dark hair. She was smaller than Grace, her head laying easily on the taller girl's shoulder. She had such a beautiful face, Emma held her hand to her mouth and gasped.

On the other side of Grace, there was a third person. In the darkness, Emma screwed her eyes together, trying to focus. It gradually became more defined, and eventually she could see it clearly.

It was a man in a collarless shirt worn by years of use, his breeches almost entirely covered by a garment fastened around his waist, rather like an apron. On his feet were heavy black boots.

Emma's eyes drifted back to his face, expecting to encounter a harsh-looking man with a steely expression, but what she saw was a kind smile. He lifted a hand to doff his cap to her. He looked every bit the proud father and a tear came to Emma's eye.

The scene took on a surreal quality as the family began to shimmer, merging together and turning as if to walk away. Just before they disappeared, Grace looked over her shoulder and blew Emma a kiss. The last thing she felt was a feathery touch on her lips, and she closed her eyes to savour the sensation. When she opened them again, the family had vanished, leaving only an immense feeling of calm. She knew then that Grace was truly at peace, reunited with both her lover and her father.

***

"You've probably opened up a gateway now. You know that, don't you?" Meredith said when Emma spoke to her the following day.

"What on earth are you talking about? I don't want to be haunted by a stream of these things!"

"You may not get any say in the matter, I'm afraid, honey. Don't worry, though. I'll be on hand to help you out when you need me."

"Gee, thanks."

The ironic tone did nothing to dispel Meredith's enthusiasm.

"Whichever way you look at it, Grace chose you, probably because of your own heartbreak, she felt you would understand her loneliness and sadness in a way that others would not. Maybe other lost spirits will find their way to you too."

"Well, I'm in no great hurry for that, you know. So, don't go sending any advertisements into the astral plane, okay? I could use some rest now, if it's all the same to you."

Meredith chuckled. "I think you need to concentrate on your own romantic life, anyway."

Emma nudged her friend playfully. This was exactly how they had been as college friends, sorting out each other's love lives, sharing their deepest and darkest secrets. Suddenly, it felt like she had turned a corner, and life was a whole lot brighter when seen from this angle.

THE END

Acknowledgmements

First and foremost, my thanks must go to my editor, Robert Doran. Your insights and encouragement alone have formed a critical part of my writing journey. Without you, this book would never have been what it has become. Thank you.

Heartfelt gratitude must also go to Katherine Bolton at The Write Retreat in Brittany, France, for granting me the solace and sanctuary to write a large part of this book. Your friendship is the sort which nourishes and sustains the soul, and it continues to humble and inspire me.

I must also mention Birdy Blacksmith in Oxfordshire for allowing me to spend a fascinating morning with him, learning about his trade and watching him work. His forge has been in existence for over four hundred years and as soon as I entered the building, I could imagine Grace's father hammering away at horseshoes on his anvil. It was the perfect inspiration.

Having the confidence to pick up my pen and write has been down, in no small part, to the Swanwick Writers Summer School which meets each August. This diverse community of writers, young and old, feels like an extended family to me. Courses on all sorts of writing-related matters, delivered by some of the most talented writers I have met, and those wonderfully cosy chats by the bar, mean that this event is now a permanent feature in my calendar. Long may this continue.

Finally, I must thank the person who, many years ago, bestowed upon me a love and appreciation of books. A lady who introduced an eager toddler to that most wonderful of institutions: the library. Before I started school, my mother took me by the hand and showed me the wonder and delight of stories, and it has never, ever left me. I hope this modest achievement goes some way towards repaying the greatest of gifts.

CPSIA information can be obtained
at www.ICGtesting.com
Printed in the USA
LVOW04s2017211016

509751LV00010B/1088/P

9 781517 191337